NO MORE HIDING

OAK BROOK ACADEMY, BOOK 3

JILLIAN ADAMS

JILLIANADAMS.COM

ONE

I stood at the end of the hallway and stared down at the noisy, clumsy teenagers that populated Oak Brook Academy. Just being around that many people was difficult for me but being smashed together with them between lockers made me want to turn around and run the other way. Still, I put one foot in front of the other and made my way toward my first class. As long as I didn't make eye contact, I was sure that I would be mostly ignored and could avoid any kind of unwanted conversation.

About halfway down the hallway, I heard a familiar voice.

"Apple! Apple! Wait up!" Chuckles chased me down and wrapped me up in an enthusiastic hug.

"Too much, too much!" I grunted as I wriggled out of his arms. "What have I told you about that?"

"I'm sorry." He grinned. "You looked so alone and small."

"I'm not small." I glared at him. "People come in all different shapes and sizes."

"Yes, and yours just happens to be fun size." He laughed.

"Shut up!" I rolled my eyes. I hadn't grown much past five feet. It made my already petite frame appear even tinier.

However, what I lacked in size I more than made up for in attitude. "Is there something you wanted?"

"Maby asked me to grab you before you got into class. She'll be here in a minute." He glanced past me at another girl in the hallway. "Vanessa! Hey there! Yes, I see you!" He waved to her.

I sighed and did my best to ignore him. Chuckles had some good qualities, but most of the time his exuberant behavior left me wanting to crawl into a hole to get away from him.

The moment I spotted Maby walking in my direction, I bolted toward her. Anything to get away from Chuckles.

"What's up?"

"Sorry to send Chuckles, but I wanted to catch you before you got into class. I collected a few boxes of art supplies for your kids. They'll be in the common room if you want to grab them before you go this afternoon." She smiled.

"A few boxes?" My eyes widened. "Wow, I didn't expect that! Thanks so much, Maby! The kids will be excited."

"Well, you just have to know how to talk to people." Maby grinned. "I'm pretty skilled at getting people to give me what I want."

"I've noticed." I stared at her with admiration. Maby had such a confidence about her, as if she could take on the world. Sometimes I wished I could steal just a little bit of it for myself. "It's perfect timing too. I have to clean out all of the old stuff this afternoon."

"I can't believe you spend every afternoon with a bunch of kids." Maby scrunched up her nose. "Don't they ever annoy you?"

"Not really." I shrugged. "I think kids are great. They say what they mean and I don't feel so nervous around them." I lowered my eyes. Even with Maby, I felt pretty shy.

"I can understand that, I guess." Maby glanced past me at a boy further down the hall. "Wes! I need to talk to you and Fi!

No disappearing on me!" She waved at him, then looked back at me. "I'm sorry, I've got to catch up with him."

"No problem. Thanks again." I turned back toward my classroom and collided with another friend. "Oh, Candy, I'm so sorry!" I caught her by the arm before she could slam into the locker behind her.

"It's okay, I don't mind being pushed around by you, little sister." She winked at me as she straightened up.

"Thanks." I gave her a quick hug. Candy and I had been friends for a long time, and in many ways, we did act more like sisters. "Hey, are you free this afternoon? I might need some help getting some supplies to the art program."

"I can't, sorry. Detention." She cringed. "Me and my mouth again. Maybe Chuckles could help you?" She grinned.

"Don't even think it!" I groaned. "I'm sure I can find somebody; don't worry about it."

A loud bell rang through the hallway. It was the first warning to get to class.

"I'd better get going before I end up with another detention." Candy rolled her eyes and hurried off.

Although Candy and I had been roommates since we started attending Oak Brook Academy as freshmen, she and I led very different lives when it came to school. She had a tendency to be late, leave everything to the last minute, and run her mouth whenever she was challenged by a teacher. She spent half of her afternoons in detention.

Me, on the other hand? I'd never even been in the principal's office and I preferred to keep it that way. Most of my school day was spent trying to go as unnoticed as possible. Aside from a close-knit group of friends, I kept to myself. It was easier that way. Whenever someone found out who I was, their entire attitude toward me would change. I'd endured enough of that to know that I was better off being invisible.

Still, there was one class I did look forward to attending each day. Art class. Mrs. Ruby, the art teacher, had struck a deal with me at the beginning of the year. She would leave me alone and I could create whatever I wanted. However, I had to promise to submit one art project per year to the art show. I agreed on the condition that it would be an anonymous submission.

Mrs. Ruby always pushed me to join the special arts program that the elite boarding school offered, but I wasn't ready for that. I preferred to keep my art private, and I certainly didn't feel confident enough to be in a special program. Not to mention the fact that my mother had indicated more than once that she wasn't paying tuition for me to splash paint on a canvas.

Unfortunately, art was just about the only thing I excelled at. Everything else was a struggle.

I pulled open the door to the classroom and stepped inside. Rows of easels filled a large open space. Several students were already perched on stools and playing with their ongoing paintings.

I walked up beside one of them.

"Oh wow, Alana, that is looking really nice. I like what you did with the color here." I pointed out a glimmer of light that she'd created on a calm surface of water.

"Thanks. I worked on that for awhile." She sighed and then smiled. "Art still isn't my thing, but I can see why you enjoy it."

"Do you think you can help me out this afternoon? Maby collected some boxes of supplies for the art program, but there's no way I can get them there on my own."

"I'm sorry, I wish I could, but Mick and I are going straight to the city after school. He wants me to meet his dad." She shook her head. "I'm not sure how that's going to go, but I guess we'll find out."

"I think that's wonderful. I'm sure you'll get along great." I gave her shoulder a quick pat and smiled.

"Maybe we could run the boxes over real quick for you?"

"Don't worry about it, I'm sure I'll find someone to help. Good luck today." I walked over to my own easel, which was in the back corner of the classroom close to a window. I'd been working on a painting for a while.

As I lifted the cloth off the canvas, I smiled at the sight of it. I was about halfway through the structure of the building and had been adding tiny details to the windows and the surrounding buildings. I had a long way to go, but I liked the progress I'd made.

"Alright everyone, eyes up here!" Mrs. Ruby clapped her hands together. "Today, I want to talk about a piece of art submitted by one of our students for the art show last year. It's a spectacular work and I'd like to get all of your opinions on it." She picked up a small canvas and placed it on the easel at the front of the class.

My heart dropped as I recognized the work that I'd created.

TWO

As Mrs. Ruby discussed my painting, I wished that I could be anywhere else. It felt strange to have people comment on it as she asked them questions.

"You're right, Alana, I think the cloud formations and the shadow of the bird create an almost three-dimensional effect. My question is, does that enhance this painting or take away from it?" She met my eyes as I tried to duck behind my easel. "Apple, what do you think?"

My heart pounded as all of the attention in the room turned toward me.

"I don't know." I frowned as I picked up my paintbrush and began to add a few touches to the painting in front of me. I had no idea why she had decided to do this, but already I had plenty to say about it—just not in front of the rest of the class.

As the discussion continued, I did my best to tune it out. Whatever her reason for this was, I didn't have to be part of it if I didn't want to.

I'd spent most of my life checking out when things made me uncomfortable. It was easier than confronting the uncomfortable feelings that upset my stomach and made my cheeks grow hot.

I tuned Mrs. Ruby out so much that when she walked toward my easel, I barely noticed that it was her behind me. When she paused beside me, I jumped and looked over at her.

"Apple, I hope you're not too upset with me." She kept her voice low.

I noticed that the other students had begun to work on their projects. The focus was no longer on my painting and I hoped that it would not be on me either.

"I don't understand why you did that." I met her eyes. "I thought we had a deal."

"We did—we do." She smiled as she looked over the painting in front of me. "Apple, it's hard for me to ignore your talent. I think maybe if you get used to people seeing your art—to hearing comments about it—you might be more willing to join the arts program or at least claim some of your paintings."

"No, I'm sorry." I sighed as I looked back at my painting. "I love to create, Mrs. Ruby, but that's all I love. I don't want the attention. I don't want the criticism." I glanced at her. "Can't I just have one thing that is just mine? I don't want to have to share it."

"It's your choice." She nodded as she stared at me. "But I do wish you would consider other options. In fact, if you'd like me to discuss it with your parents—"

"No!" I started to say more, but the door to the classroom swung open and another student strode in. I felt some relief that Mrs. Ruby was distracted by his presence. It was Ty, a pretty good friend of my friend Mick.

"Excuse me for a moment, Apple." She pointed at me. "This is not over."

I forced a smile. Mrs. Ruby had been pushing me a little bit each day in an attempt to get me to show my work with my name attached to it. But I didn't want to. She had no idea how stubborn I could be. But she would figure it out by the end of the year, that was for sure.

Curious, I watched as she walked over to Ty.

He wore a baggy hoodie that covered most of his long blond hair. His uniform pants were worn and faded in places. Was that just skater style? I'd seen him skateboarding around the courtyard. He always had a hoodie on, even though it wasn't really allowed. Maybe he thought it made him look cool. To me, it was just a sloppy style.

As I swept a paintbrush across the painting in front of me, I listened to the conversation between Mrs. Ruby and Ty.

"Can I help you with something?"

"Uh, I'm supposed to be in this class now." Ty held out a piece of paper.

"Oh? I hadn't been told about this. The class is already full. But I'm sure Principal Carter has his reasons."

"I guess." He cleared his throat.

"Okay, well, we'll get you an easel and you can get started on something. Before we get to that, though, I need to discuss a few things with you." She gestured for him to follow her up to the front of the classroom.

Once they walked past me, I watched the two head toward the front of the class. It seemed odd to me that a student would be transferred into a full class. I couldn't help but wonder why it had happened. But I also didn't care too much. As long as he left me alone and kept Mrs. Ruby occupied, he was welcome to stay.

I lost myself in the process of creating the next section of the building. I knew all of its cracks and discolorations. I wanted to make sure I didn't miss any of them. I added the hornet's nest tucked beneath one of the upper windowsills. After a few minutes, I decided to shift gears and work on some of the bushes and trees in the background of the painting. After choosing the perfect shade of green, I used careful touches of the paintbrush to create each tiny leaf.

Detail mattered to me. They always had. I found beauty in the smallest things, from a pebble among rocks to a minuscule bud on the thinnest branch of a scraggly bush.

It wasn't long before I forgot all about my painting and all about the new boy in class. In fact, I forgot all about being in a class.

Instead, my mind settled on the painting. I strolled around the bushes and trees I'd created in search of any detail that I'd missed. A cracked piece of bark here, a nearly hidden nest there. I could hear the mama bird chirping, warning me not to get too close. I could smell the fresh air laced with a hint of rain. That thought made me look up at the sky. The clouds—they should be fuller, heavier, darker. I lifted my paintbrush to the sky and began to recreate it.

When the bell rang, I nearly dropped my paintbrush as I was jolted out of my imagination.

"That was your painting, wasn't it, Apple?" Alana stared at me.

I blinked. I hadn't even realized that she'd been standing next to me.

"What painting?"

"You know what painting." She rolled her eyes. "It's gorgeous. You should show it off!"

"Thanks." I covered up the painting I had been working on and began to gather my paintbrushes to clean them.

"Not that you're going to listen to me." Alana crossed her arms. "Are you sure you're going to be okay with those boxes? I could come help you, Mick won't mind."

"No, it's fine." I smiled. "I'll figure it out. Don't worry. Good luck with Mick's dad."

"Thanks." Alana shivered. "I'm so nervous!" She groaned as she walked out of the classroom.

Once my paintbrushes were clean, I grabbed the bottle of green paint that I'd been using and picked up the cap to close it. I turned toward the shelf where the paint was stored without much thought as to who might be in my way. Most of the time I was the last to clean up.

Distracted with thoughts of the painting, I walked right into someone. The bottle of paint squished between our chests and squirted splashes of green paint up into our faces.

"Ugh!" Ty gasped as a glob of paint landed on his cheek.

"Watch it!" I huffed, then winced as paint splattered all over my cheeks and neck. It was cold and sticky. It wasn't as if I hadn't been covered in paint before, but this was entirely unexpected. Of course, it was Ty who got in my way. "Unbelievable!"

THREE

"I'm sorry." He mumbled the words as he grabbed a rag from my easel and tried to wipe some of the paint off of my cheeks and neck. I could feel the paint smear across my skin as I pulled away from him.

"Ugh, don't!" I pushed his hand away. "That's covered in paint!" I wiped at my neck, then looked at my palm. A rainbow of paint covered my skin. "Look, you've just made it so much worse!"

"I'm sorry, it was an accident." He frowned as he dropped the rag back on the easel. Specks of green covered the skin under his light blue eyes.

I glared at him as I grabbed a roll of paper towels. "Here." I pulled some of the towels off the roll and held them out to him.

"Thanks." He took the paper towels. He tore one off, then began to reach for my neck with it.

"No! Use it to clean yourself!" I took a step back and stared at him.

"Oh right, sorry," he mumbled again, then began to wipe at his face with the paper towels. He only succeeded in spreading the paint all over his skin.

"Look at you." I shook my head as I sighed. "Here, let me help." I reached up with my paper towel and rubbed the paint clean.

"Ouch!" He glared at me as he ducked his head away. "Do you have to be so rough about it?"

"Do you want to stay green?" I tossed the paper towel into the trash. "I guess maybe you do."

"It's better than getting my skin rubbed off." He frowned.

I rolled my eyes and scrubbed at my own skin. "It's the only way to get it off. You have to act fast or it will stain your skin for a few days."

"Here, let me help you with that." He raised an eyebrow as he balled up a paper towel and took a step toward me.

"Back off." I stared hard into his eyes. "I know how to clean paint off, thanks very much. Because *I* belong in an art class."

"Really?" He smirked as he looked past me at my easel. "Let's have a look and find out." He grabbed the corner of the cloth that covered my painting.

"Don't you dare!" I grabbed his hand by the wrist before he could get a hold of the cloth. I also succeeded in smearing more green paint all over his hand and sleeve.

"What's wrong?" He pulled his hand free. "I thought you belonged in an art class?" His tone sharpened. "And by the way, princess, you are the one who bumped into me."

"I was going to put my paint away!" I stood between him and my easel. The last thing I wanted was his eyes roaming all over my painting.

"And you weren't looking where you were going!" He snapped each word at me as he grabbed some more paper towel to clean off his wrist. "I apologized to be polite, because it's the right thing to do, but you are the one that walked right into me. So where is my apology?"

"You bumped into me! You should have been able to see me

walking toward you. All you had to do was step out of the way and all of this could have been avoided." I wiped at my face a little more, then sighed as I realized the paint had already begun to dry. "Great, now I'm going to be green for the rest of the day."

"Oh, trust me, if I'd seen you, I would have avoided you." He glared at me, then turned back toward the shelf of paint. "And I will do my best to avoid you from now on."

Annoyed, and more than a little tempted to tell him exactly what I thought about him, I turned back to my painting and tried to restrain myself. Accidents did happen—I knew that—and if I was honest with myself, I even knew that I hadn't been looking or paying attention when I walked toward the paint shelf. But that didn't change the fact that if he hadn't shown up in class, it never would have happened.

I glanced over at him as he lined the paints up on the shelf.

As he started to turn around, I turned back to my painting again. I pretended to be cleaning my brushes, which were already clean. Anything to avoid speaking to him.

The other students had emptied out of the classroom. I lingered by my painting, a little concerned that he might try to do something to it. Or at least take a look without my permission. I would wait until he left, just to make sure.

"Oh my, what happened to you two?" Mrs. Ruby walked up to us. "Some kind of paint war?"

"He bumped into me." I glanced over at Ty, then looked back at the teacher. "We bumped into each other."

"Right." Ty crossed his arms. I noticed that his wrist was still green and so was part of the sleeve of his hoodie.

"Ty, I do hope you're not going to cause trouble in this class." Mrs. Ruby studied him. "This is your second chance and I expect you to take full advantage of it."

He lowered his eyes as he clenched his jaw.

I waited for him to tell the truth, that it was my fault we were both covered in paint. Instead, he just nodded.

"I will." He glanced up at me, then looked away sharply.

My cheeks warmed as I realized that I had likely gotten him into trouble. But what did it matter? It sounded like he was already in trouble. As far as I knew, Ty was always in trouble, despite the fact that he had been given such a great opportunity to attend one of the most elite schools in New York, free of charge.

"Good. I'm glad to hear that." Mrs. Ruby smiled. "You can start by fulfilling some of your community service hours."

"I've been looking for somewhere to do them." Ty cleared his throat.

"Great, look no further!" Mrs. Ruby grinned as she looked over at me. "Ty, meet Apple. Apple, meet Ty. Apple runs an amazing arts program for kids every afternoon. I think it would be the perfect way for you to get some of your hours in and I'm sure that Apple could use the help. Right?" She met my eyes.

"Uh, no." I shook my head.

"I don't think that's such a good idea, Mrs. Ruby." Ty narrowed his eyes.

"Listen, I know that you two may not know each other very well. I'm sure you have different circles." She glanced between us, then shrugged. "But that's why this is perfect. It's good to get to know people who are different from you. Right, Apple?"

"Maybe, but this is not going to work." I frowned. "I prefer to work alone with the kids."

"I know you do, but the principal at the school would like to add more kids to the program and she can't do that unless you have a second volunteer to supervise. It's really worked out to be perfect timing, don't you think?" She smiled again.

I noticed for the first time that Mrs. Ruby smiled way too much.

"Actually, I have a few people in mind who might be able to help me out if that's the case. I'm sure Ty can find something else to do. Something more suited to him."

"What's that supposed to mean?" He looked over at me.

"Nothing." I shrugged. "Aren't there some homeless skateboarders you can hang out with or something?"

"Apple!" Mrs. Ruby wasn't smiling anymore.

"I just mean that he should follow his interests." I smiled.

"Actually, I think this would be perfect for me." He turned to Mrs. Ruby with a wide smile. "I'd love to work with Apple and the kids. When can I start?"

"Wonderful!" Mrs. Ruby clapped her hands together. "I just knew this would work out. I'm sure you could use the help this afternoon, right, Apple?"

I looked at Ty and saw a gleam of amusement in his eyes as he continued to smile sweetly.

Oh, he was enjoying this.

FOUR

"I don't think this is going to work." I crossed my arms as I looked between the two of them. "You know these kids need some extra attention, Mrs. Ruby. I don't think it's fair to ask so much from Ty. I'm sure there's something else for him to do."

"Actually, there isn't. He needs these hours completed by the end of the month or his scholarship will be in jeopardy." Mrs. Ruby frowned. "Don't you think you could give him a chance and see if it can work out?"

I stared at Ty. The last thing I wanted to do was give him a chance. In fact, if I never had to see him again, I would be thrilled. But I knew that if I turned Mrs. Ruby down, I would look like the bad guy and the only reason I was allowed to run the program was because of her.

"Sure." I spoke through gritted teeth. How bad could one afternoon be? I needed help with the boxes anyway. At least I could use him for some manual labor and then we could both move on.

"Wonderful. I'll leave you two to work this out, but don't take too long." She glanced at the clock on the wall. "You both need to get to your next class."

"Yes, Mrs. Ruby." I held back a sigh as she walked away.

"It's a date then?" Ty grinned at me.

"Stop." I glared at him. "I don't know what kind of game you're playing, but this program is not something I will let anyone play with. I need some help moving some boxes this afternoon, so you can come today, but that's it. Understand?"

"I'm not playing any kind of game." His grin faded into a more serious expression. "I'm the one with everything on the line here, not you. I need these hours if I'm going to stay here."

"Am I supposed to feel sorry for you?" I shook my head. "Obviously you did something wrong to get yourself into this mess. Maybe if you valued what you've been given in the first place, you wouldn't have to do this."

"Wow." He tilted his head to the side as he stared at me. "You just know everything there is to know about me, don't you?"

"I know that you're ungrateful." I watched as a few strands of his hair tumbled free of his hoodie and drifted across one light blue eye. "I think that's about all I need to know."

"I guess it is." His tone hardened. "You don't have to like me —Peach, was it? You just have to count my hours."

"Apple." I glared at him. There was no doubt in my mind that he knew exactly what my name was. It wasn't the first time that someone had teased me about my name and it wouldn't be the last, but it did speak to his maturity. "If you put in the work, I'll count your hours. Meet me right after school in the common room of the dorms. I won't wait for you if you don't show up. The kids count on me being there on time."

"Oh, I'll be there." He stared into my eyes. "And also, I'm still waiting on that apology."

"Keep waiting." I rolled my eyes, then crossed my arms. "Don't you have a class to get to?"

"Don't you?" He raised an eyebrow as the warning bell rang.

"Yes, I do, but *I'm* not going to get kicked out of school if I'm late. Are you?" I couldn't hide the faint smirk that settled on my lips.

He narrowed his eyes, then winced as the next bell rang. He turned and bolted out of the room.

As soon as the door to the classroom closed, I sighed. Every muscle in my body ached from the tension that had been pent up inside of them. I'd never met anyone who got under my skin the way that Ty seemed to.

Now I was stuck with him.

Luckily, I knew he wouldn't last the day with me. The question was, would I last the day with him?

Aggravated, I headed for the restroom to try to wash off some more of the paint that had splattered on me. As I stood in front of the sink running the hot water, I tried to calm down.

"It's free help. It's one day. It's not that big of a deal." As I spoke to my own reflection, I could see the annoyance in my expression. Yes, he really did get to me.

Once the water was warm enough, I used some paper towels and soap to try to clean my skin. It was bad enough that my short dark hair had chosen to be frizzy yet again today, but to add to that streaks of paint across my face—well, I certainly fit the part of a crazy artist. It was hard for me to be noticed, and the thought of hearing people laugh about the paint on my face all day made me sick to my stomach.

I scrubbed my face hard until I got most of the paint off. I turned off the water and stared into my cinnamon-shaded eyes. For a moment I recalled the sight of his blond hair as it tumbled across his eye. Why did I remember that?

I tried to push the thought from my mind. Already I was about ten minutes late for class and I was tempted to just skip it. But I didn't want to get into trouble. That meant more attention than I liked. I just wanted to get through the day, the afternoon, and then start over again the next day.

I trudged out of the bathroom and down the hall to my next class. Throughout the day I tried to come up with a way to get out of spending the afternoon with Ty.

At lunch, I made my way to my usual table with my usual friends.

Candy waved to me as I approached.

"Hey, how's it going?" She peered at me, then blinked. "Why do you look a little green?"

"I couldn't get all the paint off." I sighed as I sat down beside her.

"All the paint?" Maby glanced over at me. "What happened today?"

"She squirted Ty with a bunch of paint in art class." Mick took a big bite of his sandwich.

"What? That's not what happened." I blushed. "He bumped into me."

"That's not how he tells it." Mick grinned as he looked across the table at me. "You made quite an impression on him, Apple."

"Is that so?" Fi raised her eyebrows as she smiled.

"It was awful." I groaned. "And now I'm stuck with him this afternoon."

"Stuck with him?" Wes met my eyes. "What do you mean? Is he giving you a hard time or something?"

"No, not exactly. I guess he has some kind of community service hours he has to do because he's practically a juvenile delinquent." I rolled my eyes.

"Take it easy, Ty isn't a bad guy." Mick frowned. "He gets himself into some trouble now and then, but he's harmless."

"Harmless enough to need community service hours?" I

shook my head. "Whatever. If he doesn't care about his scholarship, why should anyone else?"

"Maybe you should give him a chance." Fi frowned. "It can be overwhelming to come here on a scholarship."

"Where is Alana? She would stand up for me if she were here. She probably saw the whole thing." I sighed.

"We'll always stand up for you, Apple." Candy nudged me with her shoulder. "But Fi is right, sometimes being an outsider can be really hard at a school like this."

"Trust me, he's no wounded soul." I narrowed my eyes as I recalled how sweet he'd acted toward Mrs. Ruby. "It doesn't matter anyway. We're only going to work together for one afternoon. After that, he's not my problem anymore." I took a bite of my food and tried to forget all about Ty.

But again, that memory of his stupid hair falling over his stupid eye interrupted my thoughts.

FIVE

As the last class of the day finished up, I felt an immense dread.

Maybe Ty just wouldn't show up. From what I knew of him, he wasn't a very reliable person. Anytime I saw him in the courtyard, he was off on his own or skating. He didn't seem to be too interested in making friends. He and Mick had gotten close because they were both on the football team. Other than that, though, I hadn't noticed him with anyone else. Then again, I hadn't really noticed him.

Before that morning I hadn't thought twice about him, now I couldn't get him out of my head.

I headed straight for the common room and found the boxes that Maby had left for me. I felt immediate relief that I might have help when I saw the size of them. They weren't exactly light either. Getting them to the school would be difficult even with Ty's help—if he bothered to show up.

Of course he wouldn't, I reminded myself. He would expect me to just sign off on his hours. It was tempting to do just that—just to have him out of my hair. But the truth was, I really needed his help that afternoon.

As the minutes ticked by, I grew more and more impatient.

How hard was it to be on time? He didn't have to make much of an effort—just show up and move a couple of boxes. But no, he wasn't even capable of that.

I walked the length of the common room and did my best to avoid eye contact with the other kids hanging out there. They'd seen me waiting. They knew that someone wasn't showing up for me.

I glanced at my watch again. I couldn't wait any longer. I had to get going or I would be late to the program and the kids would have to miss it because there would be no one there to supervise them.

The more I thought about it, the more my anger increased. If he hadn't said he would be there, I could have arranged for someone else to help me. Now it was too late.

Annoyed, I stacked up two of the boxes. Maybe if I could get them out the door, I could get the other one the next day. As I tried to lift them, I cringed at how heavy they were. I'd never been an athletic person. It just wasn't something I enjoyed. A good walk through the park or a swim now and then was fine, but vigorous exercise was generally off the table. The truth was, I just wasn't that strong.

As soon as I picked the boxes up, my entire body began to sway. I stumbled backward a few steps, then forward. I could barely see over the top of the boxes that I tried to carry. As I swayed back again, I almost lost my balance and leaned forward in an attempt to keep it without dropping the boxes. Seconds later I was stumbling backward again and this time I could tell that I wasn't going to regain my balance. As I began to tilt further and further back, the boxes started to slide in different directions.

"Oh no!" I gulped as I felt one foot slip out from under me.

"I got you!" Ty ran toward me and managed to catch me by the shoulders before I could tumble all the way back. With the boxes pinned between us he had to stretch around them to hold onto me.

I stumbled again but managed to get both feet back on the floor.

"What are you doing?" He frowned as he took the boxes from my arms and set them down on the floor.

"I was doing just fine, thanks!" The words popped out of my mouth as I straightened myself up.

Determined to look capable, I took a step forward without realizing that the corner of one of the boxes was right in front of me. As I tripped, Ty darted to the side and easily caught me around the waist.

I reached for his shoulders in the same moment in an attempt to steady myself and ended up with my arms around his neck. I didn't have time to be mortified, as my heart raced the moment his arms were around me. It was a shock to be so suddenly close to someone, but to be near him in particular made it even more startling.

"Just fine, huh?" He smiled some as I pulled away as quickly as I could.

"I would have been, if you had been here on time." I glared at him.

"I'm sorry." He frowned. "I got caught up with Principal Carter. He wanted to talk to me about our arrangement."

"We don't have an arrangement." I pointed to the boxes on the floor. "If you can get those two, I think I can get this one."

"I'm not so sure about that." He cringed as he watched me try to pick up the last box. "I can carry all three of them if you can stack that one on top." He picked up the two boxes on the floor, then crouched down some. "Go on, pop it on top."

"I can carry it." I rolled my eyes. Then I tried to take a step forward. The box was heavier than I expected.

"Just put it up here, alright? That's the deal, isn't it? I do the heavy lifting?" He crouched down a little further. "Can you get it?"

"Yes." I huffed as I put the box on top of the first two. "There's no way you can carry all this. We'll just have to leave one box here."

"I've got it, relax." He held up the boxes a little higher. "I just have to trust you not to let me walk into anything or anyone. Can I trust you?" He peered over the top of the boxes.

All I could see were his blue eyes and the blond hair that splayed across his forehead under his hood.

"Yes, you can trust me." I put my hand on his arm and did my best to hold back my frustration. As long as he was helping me, I would try to be polite.

"I'm not so sure about that," he muttered as I led him through the door and out into the courtyard.

"Don't worry, it's not a far walk."

"Walk?" He followed after me.

I kept my hand on his arm to make sure that he didn't walk into anything, but a part of me was tempted to let him walk right off the curb when we reached the gates of the entrance to Oak Brook Academy. Instead, I pulled back on his arm to slow him down.

"Okay, now we need to get to the bus stop."

"Bus stop?" He lowered the boxes some so that he could see me clearly. "Are you messing around with me?"

"Not at all." I frowned. "Are you sure you're okay carrying all that?"

"I'm fine." He lifted the boxes back up again. "I just wish you would tell me ahead of time where we're going."

"I might have had time for that if you had been on time." I glared at him. "It really makes a bad impression to show up late, you know."

"I told you, I got delayed by the principal. Why are you giving me a hard time?"

"Never mind." I frowned. There was no point in talking to him if he didn't want to listen.

When we reached the bus stop, I checked my watch. "We're cutting it close—hopefully it didn't come early."

"Why didn't you just use a car service?" He set the boxes down on the ground.

"Why, are you too good for a bus?" I raised an eyebrow as I looked at him.

"Too good?" He rolled his eyes. "I'm pretty sure you've got that role covered."

"Oh? You think you know so much about me, hmm?" I crossed my arms as the bus pulled up.

"I know that a girl like you wouldn't normally be riding a bus." He stared into my eyes. "In fact, you probably had to learn how to when you got here. Didn't you?"

My cheeks flushed. I didn't want to admit it, but he was right. It had taken a lot for me to get on the bus for the first time.

"Just get the boxes!" I turned to face the bus as it pulled to a stop.

SIX

I heard Ty grumble behind me as I stepped up into the bus. When I turned back to help him in with the boxes, his eyes met mine. From the squint and the shadow over the light blue shade of his eyes, I gathered that he liked me about as much as I liked him.

"Right here." I pointed to one of the empty seats near the front of the bus.

"Sure." He dropped the boxes on the seat, then sat down beside them.

I took the seat across the aisle from his. "It's not far. About fifteen minutes."

"Okay." He looked past the boxes out through the side window of the bus.

As I did the same, I could hear my own words echoing through my mind. I'd been harsh. Far harsher than I normally was with anyone. It wasn't my nature to be cruel. But Ty brought something out in me that other people didn't. Why was that? I stole a glance over at him.

He continued to stare out the window but kept one hand on the boxes to hold them in place.

"So, what did you do?"

"Excuse me?" He looked over at me, then back at the window.

"What did you do to get in trouble? Did you cheat on a test? Blow up a toilet?" I slid over on the seat. The engine of the bus was loud enough to drown out his voice.

"Blow up a toilet?" He smirked as he looked at me again. "Am I a terrorist now?"

"I don't know. Are you?" I quirked an eyebrow.

"What I did is none of your business." He shrugged.

"Oh, I see. Okay, well, I don't really care either way, I was just making conversation."

"You don't do that much, do you?" He squinted at me.

"Do what?"

"Make conversation. I've seen you around. I hardly ever hear you talk."

"I talk. To certain people."

"Not me, I guess."

"I'm talking to you now, aren't I?" I crossed my arms as I tried to get my nerves under control. He managed to annoy me no matter what he said.

"Because you feel obligated. Not because you actually want to." He tipped his head toward the front of the bus. "This program you're running, what's the point of it?"

"I believe all children should have access to art. This program ensures that there is a place for them to create."

"Seems like a good thing to do." He studied me. "Is that why you do it? Just because it's good? It'll look great on your college applications."

"No." I pursed my lips. I could sense the judgment in his voice.

"Sure it is. You're smart enough to have a motive behind everything you do."

The bus lurched to a stop.

"You have no idea what you're talking about." I stood up and walked off the bus.

As I waited for him to struggle and stumble down the steps with the three boxes, I resisted the urge to help him. If he wanted to insult me, I would let him work hard to get those hours of community service in.

"So, enlighten me." He grunted as he shifted the boxes in his arms. "Why are you wasting your time on something like this?"

"It's not a waste of time." I led him into the school and down the hall toward the classroom that I used. "If you think it is, then you shouldn't be here."

"Please, don't expect me to believe that you're doing all this out of the kindness of your heart." He dropped the boxes onto the floor in front of the door.

"You know what, you can just go now." I shoved the boxes through the door into the classroom. "I've got it from here."

"What?" He ducked his head to the side to catch my eyes. "I need these hours. You heard what Mrs. Ruby said."

"You need these hours because you messed up, so don't expect me to feel bad for you." I began to pull supplies out of one of the boxes.

"Apple, we had a deal." He stepped into the classroom as well. The door snapped closed behind him.

I glanced up at him as I realized that we were alone.

"I don't expect you to understand this, but this is my favorite place to be." I looked into his eyes. "I come here because it's what I love to do. Being around these kids—it's not hours on a sheet of paper for me. It's a place where I can feel calm, where I can be myself. I don't want that getting ruined."

"I'm not going to ruin it." He held my gaze. "I'm not sure why you think I would, but I'm not going to."

"We argued from the time we left the school until now.

Does that sound peaceful to you?" I grabbed another handful of supplies.

"I don't want to stress you out." He pushed his hood back off of the top of his head and took a deep breath. "Just give me a chance. I can help you out."

"I don't need your help." I stacked some paint on one of the nearly empty shelves in the closet that the school allowed me to use.

"I know you don't." He set a bottle of paint on the shelf beside the ones I stacked. "But I need your help, Apple. I know you don't think much of me and that's fine. I don't need you to. But right now, you're my only chance to stick around at Oak Brook."

"So what?" I turned to face him. "It seems to me that you don't like it here much anyway. You're always getting yourself into some kind of trouble, always sulking."

"Sulking?" His eyes narrowed, then he shook his head. "You're right, I do get myself into some tough spots. But that doesn't mean I don't know what kind of advantage this is."

"You don't act like you know it." I grabbed some sponges and paintbrushes. "I just don't think it's a good idea for us to work together. Kids can sense tension."

"I'll stay out of your way. I won't argue." He frowned. "I promise."

I stared at him for a moment. As tough as he acted, at that moment, he appeared to be begging for my help. Did I really want to turn down an extra pair of hands when there were a ton of supplies to put away and the kids would arrive at any minute?

"Fine." I sighed. "You can stay. But you're only going to help with storing the supplies and cleaning. I don't want you interacting with the kids. Understand?" I locked my eyes to his.

"Why? Do you think I'm a bad influence?" He frowned.

"See?" I shook my head as I walked back over to the boxes.

"Okay, okay, forget I said it." He walked over behind me and picked up one of the boxes. "I've got this. I'm sure that you have stuff to do to prepare for the kids getting here. I'll stay in the background. You won't hear a word from me. I promise." He smiled and held up one hand. "You won't even know I'm here."

"I doubt that." I began to set up the easels for each of the students. It was exciting to think that the school wanted to add more students, but there was no way I could be paired up with Ty, no matter what Mrs. Ruby had to say.

When the door to the classroom burst open, I turned to greet the kids with a bright smile.

"Welcome, everyone! Come in, come in, tell me about your day." I greeted each one in turn by name and listened as they told me about their day at school. They ranged in age from eight to eleven, and although most were quite thrilled to be part of the class, some weren't. One in particular, I'd been working with for over a month. At ten, he was one of the must sullen little people I'd ever met and he had a temper. I had to be careful with him or he would lose it.

"How are you doing today, Patrick?" I smiled at him.

He stared at me, then walked over to his easel. I was used to his ignoring me. But I still always tried to reach out.

"Alright, everyone, I've got great news." I sat on the edge of the desk in the front of the room. "We have some new supplies for us to use. It's important to remember that we need to take care of our supplies. Put the caps back on. Don't leave the paints scattered around the room. Okay?"

"Who's that?" A nine-year-old named Bianca pointed at Ty in the back of the room.

SEVEN

"Let's just focus on our project." I smiled. "So remember, we're working on a painting of our favorite animal or whatever you would like to create. If you want any help with your painting, let me know." I walked among the easels, checking to be sure that each student had what they needed.

As usual, Patrick sat at his easel and stared at a blank canvas.

"Do you want to check out some of our new supplies, Patrick?" I paused beside him. "There might be something that you'd like to try out in there."

He glared at me, then looked back at the empty canvas.

As I moved on to the next child, I noticed that Patrick actually picked up one of his paintbrushes. I did my best not to show how excited I was, but my heart raced. Maybe he was finally ready to create something.

"Bianca, that's a very nice bunny tail." I paused beside her canvas. "I like all the fluff you put into it."

"Thanks." She smiled. "But it needs glitter."

"Ah yes, everything needs glitter, right?" I grinned at her.

"Maybe." She laughed.

"It's your bunny, it can have a glittery tail if you want it to." I moved on to the next child but glanced back over my shoulder at Patrick. As I watched, he began to poke and swipe at his canvas. He punctuated each movement with a grimace or a sneer.

"Would you like some help, Patrick?" I walked over to him. "There are certain techniques you can try, different strokes that will create different effects on the canvas."

"No!" He glared at me, then threw his paintbrush across the room. When it hit the floor, paint splattered across the tiles. He stared at it for a long moment.

"Patrick, you're going to have to clean that up." I frowned. "You don't have to paint if you don't want to, but throwing the paintbrushes isn't acceptable."

"No, no, no!" he shouted at me as he stomped away from his easel.

I gritted my teeth. I didn't want to have to call the principal to intervene. The other students all watched him with wide eyes. My stomach twisted as I thought of times in my life that everyone had stared at me for one reason or another. It had never been easy.

"Alright, everyone, back to work." I strolled among the easels and ignored Patrick, who continued to stomp around the back of the room. Maybe if I gave him some time, he would calm down.

As I turned back to check on him, I spotted Ty on his knees with a rag.

"Ty, what are you doing?" I walked over to him as he wiped up the paint from the tiles.

"Cleaning up." He glanced up at me. "That's what I'm here for, right?"

"Right, but I asked Patrick to clean it up."

"He's not going to." He looked over at the boy.

Patrick crossed his arms as he glared at both of us.

"You didn't give him a chance to." I sighed. "Kids need to be held responsible for their actions."

"Oh?" He stood up with the paintbrush in his hand. "I thought this place was for creating art?"

"It is." I narrowed my eyes.

"So, now you're upset with him for creating?"

"I'm not upset." I shook my head. "What are you talking about? He didn't create anything."

"Sure he did." He pointed to some of the paint still splattered on a nearby chair. "That looks like art to me."

I rolled my eyes. "Forget it." As I started to walk away, I caught sight of Ty as he strolled over to Patrick.

"Hey, buddy. I'm Ty." He pulled a chair over and sat down beside Patrick.

"So?" Patrick glared at him.

"So, I like what you did there." He smiled.

I balled my hands into fists. Just as I expected, he was a bad influence. How could he encourage such out-of-control behavior? I opened my mouth to correct him, but Patrick spoke up before I could.

"You do?" Patrick stared at him.

"I do." Ty held up the paintbrush in his hand. "You've got quite a talent for splatter art. Have you ever tried it on a bigger canvas?"

"Huh?" Patrick's arms settled at his sides and he stepped closer to Ty. "What do you mean?"

"I'll show you—if you want." He shrugged. "If not, it's cool."

"Show me." Patrick almost smiled.

I could only watch in shock. I'd been working with Patrick for months and he had barely spoken to me. But with Ty, he appeared relaxed and even interested.

"I'll need some help. Can you help me out?" He stood up and walked over to the supplies.

"Sure." Patrick followed after him.

Ty pulled out a roll of large paper. I used it to simulate murals for the kids.

"Take this end." He handed Patrick one end of the paper. "Now roll it all the way down to the end of the window there."

Patrick did as Ty instructed.

I braced myself for disaster, but Patrick remained engaged and curious.

Once Ty had two layers of the paper taped up on the wall he grinned at Patrick.

"Alright, I'm going to show you something, but I'll warn you, if you try this at home, your mom is going to get real mad."

"She's always mad." Patrick rolled his eyes. "Show me!"

"Okay, stand back. This is like an explosion." He grabbed a bottle of paint and poured a large amount all over the paintbrush in his hand. The excess dripped onto a drop cloth he'd spread out beneath him. "Ready?" He smiled as he looked into Patrick's eyes.

"Ready!" Patrick stood up on his toes and grinned.

The way his face lit up took my breath away.

Ty flung the paintbrush at the layers of paper on the wall. The paintbrush landed with a thud against the paper and splattered paint in all directions around it.

"Wow!" Patrick squealed and laughed. "Wow, it's like an explosion!"

"Yup." Ty picked up the paintbrush. "Now, it's your turn."

"Really?" He looked from Ty to me. "I won't get in trouble?"

"No, Patrick, you won't get in trouble. Have at it!" I smiled. It inspired me to see him excited about art.

"What if we do more than one color?" He grabbed a new paintbrush and a few bottles of paint off of the shelf. "What do you think that will be like?"

"Let's find out." Ty helped him open one of the bottles.

Then he hesitated. He met my eyes. "I mean, if that's okay with you? I know you don't want me around the kids."

As I stared into his light blue eyes I felt a flutter of something. Respect?

No, it was different. I bit into my bottom lip as I realized exactly what it was.

"It's fine. Have fun, Patrick. I can't wait to see what you create." I smiled at him.

For the first time since I'd met Patrick, he smiled back at me.

As I walked around to help the other kids, I kept an eye on Ty and Patrick. The two experimented with different colors, different size paintbrushes, and even sponges. When it was time to go, the paper was covered from one end to the other and Patrick hadn't stopped smiling. My heart soared when I heard him laugh.

As the kids headed out to catch the bus, Patrick stopped in the doorway and looked back at Ty.

"See you tomorrow, Ty?"

"Uh, we'll see, pal." Ty winked at him.

"I hope so!" Patrick waved to him, then ran out the door.

"That's up to you, isn't it?" Ty turned to look at me. The smile that he'd given to Patrick had faded and as he met my eyes, his expression darkened even further. "Do I get to come back tomorrow?"

EIGHT

My initial reaction was to get far away from Ty as fast as I could. He stirred things in me that I didn't know how to define. But what he'd done with Patrick was nothing short of magic. I could only imagine how the little boy would react if he showed up the next day and Ty wasn't there to paint with.

"How did you know?"

"How did I know what?" He stared back at me.

"How did you know how to reach Patrick? I've been trying for months."

"It wasn't hard." He shrugged.

"Oh. I guess I'm just terrible at this then?" I rolled my eyes and walked back over to the easels to clean up a few bottles of paint that had been left behind.

"I wouldn't say that." He gathered some paper towels from the floor and tossed them into a nearby trash can. "Not with the easy kids. But not all kids are easy."

"I thought he hated art. I've been trying so hard." I sighed as I turned back to face him. "But you just looked at him and knew what to do."

"No, I listened to him." He pointed to Patrick's easel.

"Sometimes having limitations can kill creativity. He doesn't like the boundaries of the canvas. And maybe holding the paintbrush is hard for him. So he thinks he can't create anything. He watches the other kids getting praise for their work and he just can't do it."

"I just thought he didn't want to." I frowned.

"All kids want to create. Well, all people, maybe?" He raised his eyebrows. "Anyway, I knew it was in there. When he threw the paintbrush, that was something that he could do. It was a way he could express his frustration. So I decided to see if he wanted to do more of it. Sometimes it's not about getting someone to do what you want but encouraging them to figure out how they are capable of doing it."

"It's just amazing." I smiled. "I could have worked with him all year and maybe he never would have had a day like this. Ty, you really reached him. That's pretty great."

"Thanks." He walked over to me, his eyes locked to mine. "Does that mean that I get to come back?"

"Yes." I took a deep breath and did my best to ignore how close he stood to me. "You can come back. But I take all this very seriously. It's not just something I do for a pat on the back. I do it because I hope it can make a difference."

"So, you still doubt me?" He shook his head. "What's it going to take to prove to you that I'm a decent human being?"

"I think what you did with Patrick is wonderful. I have no idea whether you are a decent human being or not. All I know is that you seem to have a problem with me. You also like to argue."

"I like to argue?" He offered a short laugh as he stared at me.

"All I'm saying is that this is my program, these are my kids. Yes, you can come back, as long as you are doing your best to help them and not causing them any harm."

"I would never do anything to cause them harm." He

narrowed his eyes. "If you think I would, then maybe you're right—maybe we can't work together."

"I'm not saying you would, I'm just very careful with these kids. Many of them have had it rough. I don't want to take any chances of making anything worse." I crossed my arms. "You can be annoyed with me for it, but it's not going to change."

"I'm not annoyed." He rubbed his hands together and sighed. "I think we both have the wrong impression of each other and we keep making it worse. We don't even know each other."

"We can fix that." I put away the last of the supplies then turned back to face him. "Why don't you tell me something about you?"

"Trust me, you wouldn't be interested." He followed me out through the door.

"Obviously I am." I turned back to close the door behind us and do one last check of the room to make sure nothing was out of place.

"Why? So you can feel better about having me around?" He waited for me to take the lead down the hallway.

"See, that's what I'm talking about." I looked over at him. "I thought you said we had the wrong idea about each other?"

"I thought we did, but sometimes the way you talk to me makes me feel like a toddler." He shook his head. "I'm not as much of an idiot as you seem to think."

"I don't think that." I frowned. "I'm not that good at talking to people. Okay? I'm not that used to it."

"Because it's safer to stay silent and out of the way, right?" He fell into step beside me as we headed toward the bus stop.

"I don't know if it's safer. I'm not afraid of much. But it's a lot less trouble than trying to figure out what I'm supposed to say, how I'm supposed to act."

"Aren't you ever just you?" He peered at me from under loose strands of golden hair.

"I guess that's easy for you." I glanced down the street in search of the bus.

"What's easy for me?" He perched on the edge of the bench.

"Being you. It seems like it comes easy to a lot of people. It's never come easy to me." I frowned. "Where are you from?"

"Nowhere in particular." He shrugged.

"Where do you live—when you're not at Oak Brook?" I turned to look at him.

"With my parents."

"Obviously." I narrowed my eyes. "Are you being evasive just to annoy me?"

"I answered your questions, didn't I?" He looked up at me.

"No, you didn't. I know you're here on a scholarship. Which means that you had to qualify for it. I just can't figure out how. You never seem to pay attention in class. You don't take your studies seriously."

"Wow, you know a lot about me for someone who knows absolutely nothing about me." He spread his arms across the top of the bench and stared at me. "Do tell, what are the rest of my flaws? My hair?" He flicked a strand of it. "Too long? Too blond?" He raised an eyebrow.

"I didn't say they were flaws. I was just pointing out some things that I'd observed." I crossed my arms. "Maybe if you spent more time improving yourself, you'd be less likely to be judged."

"Improving myself. There it is." He nodded. His jaw tensed as he looked in the direction of the bus that approached. When he looked back at me his lips were tight and his eyes narrowed. "Maybe if you spent less time reassuring yourself that you're better than everyone else, you wouldn't find it so hard to connect with other people." He stood up from the bench so suddenly that I didn't have time to step back before he was practically nose to nose with me. "Do you think riding the bus and painting with some poor kids gives you the right to decide who needs improvement and who doesn't?"

"I never said that. You're twisting my words." I shifted a few steps back from him. The bus hissed and squeaked as it stopped. My heart pounded as he searched my eyes.

"I'm not twisting anything. I think I'll improve myself with a nice long walk."

"Don't be ridiculous. It will take you forever!" I stared at him as he stepped away from me.

"Better than any amount of time trapped somewhere with you." He waved his hand over his head as he quickened his pace.

"Ty!" I groaned with frustration. "Get back here! The bus isn't going to wait for you!"

"Good! Make sure you get on it!" He glared over his shoulder, then strode off.

NINE

Furious, I stormed onto the bus and stomped past the driver.

"Easy now." The driver eyed me. "I don't want any trouble!"

"I'm fine, I'm sorry." I slouched down in a seat and glared out the window. How could Ty talk to me like that? Of course I didn't volunteer to make myself feel better than other people. That was such a ridiculous thing for him to say, and right after I'd begun to think that he might be decent after all.

If it weren't for the way he'd reached Patrick, I'd tell him never to come near me again. Then again, with the way he hurried off, I guessed that his being around me wouldn't be a problem. But he had reached Patrick in a way that I hadn't been able to—and that was important to me.

As my anger died down to a subtle annoyance, I thought about our conversation. He was right. We picked at each other like enemies when we barely knew each other. I had hoped that maybe we could have a friendship, especially after how helpful he'd been. But now I saw that friendship was likely impossible. We were far too different for there ever to be anything between us.

I closed my eyes and allowed the sound of the bus's engine

to lull me into a more peaceful state. As my mind drifted, memories of his eyes locked to mine filled my thoughts. Each time I pushed them away, they returned even more stubbornly.

"Ugh." I rubbed my hand across my forehead as if I could scrub him from my thoughts. Instead, I found myself thinking about the way it had felt when I'd ended up with my arms around his neck. For an instant, I'd considered what it would be like to kiss him. I didn't want to admit it, but it was true. And as I considered it again, that flutter I'd felt, after he'd helped Patrick, returned.

Once more I tried to deny what it was. I could not possibly be attracted to him. Ty was everything that I didn't like, everything that I had zero interest in.

He was ungrateful, even for the opportunity I'd given him to get his volunteer hours. He was emotional and brash, deciding to walk home instead of taking the bus because he couldn't keep his emotions under control. Clearly, he was overly sensitive and took everything I said the wrong way. There was nothing about him that would lead me to think he would be a good option to date. And yet, as soon as I closed my eyes, there he was again.

"Great." I sighed as the bus lurched to a stop. "Just great." I left the bus and headed back through the entrance of Oak Brook Academy. "I'm just going a little crazy. Everyone has been pairing up lately and it's got me feeling like I need to also." I shook my head.

"Yeah, it is a little crazy to talk to yourself." Maby laughed as she stepped up beside me. "Hey, did you get the boxes to the school okay?"

"Yes, I had some help." I frowned.

"Usually having help makes people happy." Maby quirked an eyebrow. "Is everything okay?"

"It will be once I manage to scrub my brain clean of all this romance that's running rampant around here."

"Okay?" Maby laughed. "You can always use my technique and save romance until you're older."

"I like that plan. But right now, I think I just need a shower and to get my mind on anything else."

"Wait, wait, are you saying you have a crush?" Maby grinned. "On who? You've got to tell me!"

"I do not have to tell you! I never will. Not ever." I hurried away from her.

"Oh, you're going to tell me!" Maby chased after me.

I broke into a run. The last thing I needed was to be grilled by Maby. She really could get anything out of anyone. Besides, I didn't enjoy the attention on me. I just needed to clear my head and get rid of all of the craziness that had built up inside me.

Of course it was easy to have a crush on Ty. With all that shiny hair and those bright eyes, who wouldn't find him attractive?

But I wasn't one of those people. I wasn't attracted to people based on the way they looked. In fact, I wasn't really attracted to people. Dating wasn't really top of my list of things to accomplish. I'd just settled into the idea that it would have to wait until I got a little braver. Now, I was faced with this ridiculous crush. But I wouldn't stand for it.

I managed to get to my dorm room and lock the door before Maby could catch me.

"Apple!" Maby knocked on the door. "This isn't over! I'm going to find out!" She laughed.

"What's going on?" Candy stood up from the sofa. "Aren't you going to let her in?"

"Not a chance." I flopped down next to her. "And don't you let her in either."

"Okay." Candy sat down beside me. "What's going on? Are you okay?"

I picked up a pillow and buried my face in it. "I'm not sure that I'll ever be okay again."

"What happened?" She pulled the pillow back to look at me. "Do I need to hurt someone?"

"Is that an option?" I considered it for a moment. It might solve my problem.

"It depends on who it is." Candy laughed.

"I'd rather not talk about it."

"Too bad." She yanked the pillow free of my grasp and tossed it aside. "We're going to talk about it. Every little detail."

"No." I grabbed another pillow.

"You can't keep closing yourself off this way. I'm your best friend. You need to talk to me." She tugged at my pillow.

"I will." I tossed it aside and sighed. "I'm sorry, Candy. I'm just really wiped out. Trust me, it's not a big deal; I just need some time to sort it out."

"Alright, but I'm here if you need me." She shook her head. "I hate to see you upset and feel like I can't do anything to help you."

"You can. You can keep Maby away from me. In fact, you can keep everyone away from me until I can clear my head."

"I guess I can do that." She frowned. "But I'd rather you just talked to me."

"I know. And I will." I stood up from the sofa. "I just need some time."

As I stepped into my room and closed the door, I instantly regretted it. I knew that Candy would worry about me. But I just couldn't bring myself to say out loud what I knew had taken root in my heart.

I wanted absolutely nothing to do with Ty. But I also couldn't stop thinking about him. It was the most confusing experience I'd ever had.

Yes, maybe he did have some good qualities, but that didn't

change the fact that he wasn't my type, he would never be interested in someone like me, and I wasn't sure either of us would survive being alone together. There were plenty of reasons that I had developed a crush, but far more reasons to do everything in my power to ignore it.

I hoped that a good night's sleep would change everything.

But the moment I opened my eyes the next morning, I felt that flutter. Only instead of a flutter, it was a full-out flapping. I squeezed my eyes shut tight and tried to go back to sleep and start over again. But closing my eyes only filled my thoughts with the memory of his smile and the gentle way he'd worked with Patrick.

Finally, I climbed out of bed.

After a shower, I pulled on my uniform, grabbed my books, and headed out for the day. If pretending it didn't exist wouldn't get rid of my crush, then I would just have to find another way. I knew that Ty wasn't right for me. I just needed to prove that to myself. If that meant finding out everything there was to know about Ty, then that was exactly what I would do.

By the end of the day, I'd have a million reasons not to want to be with him, and that would certainly cure me of this ridiculous crush.

TEN

I headed straight for the football field. If I wanted to know more about Ty, there was on person in particular that I could talk to.

I happened to know that Mick always ran sprints in the morning. He did his best to keep in shape for the team. I would be interrupting, but he would have to get over it. I needed to know more and he was my best option.

As I approached the field, it occurred to me that I might run into Ty as well, but I dismissed the thought. Ty didn't commit himself to anything. There was no way he would spend time before school running sprints.

As expected, I found Mick alone on the football field. I watched him run back and forth a few times, then finally he jogged over to me.

"Why are you staring at me?" He wiped some sweat from his forehead.

"I need to talk to you."

"You do? Me?" He grinned. "Are you sure you don't have me mixed up with someone else?'

"Forget it." I huffed and started to turn away.

"Wait, wait. I'm just used to you going to Maby and Candy, not me." He shrugged. "I'm listening."

"It's about Ty."

"Oh. Is it?" He cleared his throat. "Maybe I'm not the best person to talk to about that."

"Why is that?" I noticed the way he avoided my eyes. "Did he say something about yesterday?"

"Say something? Not exactly." He tipped his head back and forth. "It was more like shouting and a little bit of incoherent rambling. I mean, what did you do to him, Apple?"

"What did *I* do?" I frowned. "It's not my fault."

"I picked him up on the side of the road."

"He chose not to get on the bus." I threw my hands up in the air. "He was having a tantrum."

"A tantrum?" He grinned. "Oh, I'll bet he'd love to hear you say that."

"That's what it was. I'm telling you the truth. I told him he should get on the bus and he threw a fit and stomped off like a two-year-old."

"Ouch." He raised an eyebrow. "Maybe you should take a look behind you."

"Huh?" I glanced over my shoulder and found Ty right behind me. "What are you doing here?"

"What am I doing on the football field?" He licked his lips. "I'm not the one that doesn't belong here."

"I just thought it was a bit early for you to be out and about." I clenched my hands into fists as I dug myself deeper into a hole. Not only had he overheard me accusing him of having a tantrum, I'd also insulted him. It didn't matter much if I had a crush on him, he would clearly never want anything to do with me.

"I come out here to strengthen my speed. Mick has been

helping me with that." He eyed me for a moment, then stepped past me. "Are we doing this or not, Mick?"

"Sure. Do you two need a minute?" He looked between us.

"Not even a second." Ty glared over his shoulder at me, then took off at a run.

"Wow." Mick chuckled. "I'm sorry Apple. I guess you really got under his skin."

"Trust me, the feeling is mutual." I rolled my eyes.

"Did you still need to talk?" He glanced after Ty as he ran across the field.

"No, I'm fine. Go run." I turned and walked off the field.

I hadn't learned much more about Ty but I'd certainly been reminded of why I had to get rid of this crush.

By the time I made it to my first class, I'd worked myself into a frustrated state. I didn't want to hope that Ty would show up, but I also couldn't not hope that he would show up.

I uncovered my painting and tried to lose myself in it. Usually painting was my way to escape from everything. No matter what was on my mind, splashing some paint across a canvas could make everything better. But as I added in some details of the first floor of the building, I felt overly critical instead. Why did that line have to be a little curvy instead of straight? Why hadn't I chosen a lighter color?

I was tempted to throw the entire canvas out the window.

"Good morning, everyone, let's get started." Mrs. Ruby stood behind her desk in the front of the room. "As you know, part of our curriculum this year is studying the great artists of the past. So, I've planned a trip to a little known art museum. I know, I know, we've been to all the museums around the city, but I'll bet this one is one you've never been to. I'm going to let it be a surprise. But we'll be going this Friday. So please make sure that you are free that day. I'm really excited about this and I think you're going to love it."

I focused on her words. A field trip sounded like a good distraction. Maybe if I immersed myself in some excellent art, I'd be able to forget all about Ty's effect on me.

Just then the classroom door swung open and Ty stepped inside.

"Ty, you're late." Mrs. Ruby placed her hands on her hips.

"Sorry, Mrs. Ruby, I got caught up with the coach." He walked over to his easel without ever looking in my direction.

"I'll let it slide, but just this once. Art class is just as important as any other class you're in. Apple, will you fill him in about the trip, please? The rest of you, please take out a fresh canvas. We're going to work on something new today." She set a bowl of fruit on her desk where everyone could see.

A few students groaned.

"Don't worry. It's not what you think." She grinned. "It's easy to look at this bowl of fruit and see the fruit. You can see the colors, the shapes. But I want you to paint what you can't see. I want you to paint their taste, their smell." She picked up an orange and sniffed it. "It may seem strange to think of painting a taste or smell, but being able to communicate all five senses through art is what sets an artist apart from someone who can draw a pretty picture."

I glanced over at Ty. The last thing I wanted to do was talk to him. But Mrs. Ruby had asked me to do something, and as she was my favorite teacher, I did my best not to upset her.

"So, we're going on a trip to a museum on Friday."

Ty nodded again without looking at me. "Which museum?"

"It's a surprise." I picked up a fresh canvas.

"Mocking me again?" He sighed and looked at me only long enough to glare.

"No, I'm serious." I set the canvas on the easel. "Mrs. Ruby is keeping it a surprise."

"Great." He picked up a canvas again. "That sounds about as fun as this assignment. Paint taste?"

"There's no need to be rude. She's a great teacher."

"There's no need to tell me what to do, is there?" He again looked in my direction, only this time he glared at me a little longer.

"Don't worry, if it's too hard for you, you can always paint a football." I rolled my eyes.

"You are ridiculous!" He stood up from his stool, turned, then walked right back through the classroom door.

"Ty?" Mrs. Ruby watched him go. "Where are you going? Class just started! Ty!"

I sank down on my stool. There he went again. Getting himself into trouble. I bit into my bottom lip as I tried to paint the taste of a banana. Was it maybe just a little bit my fault this time?

My heart pounded at the thought. No, I didn't want to have a crush on him, but that didn't mean I wanted to get him kicked out of school either.

ELEVEN

I didn't see Ty for the rest of the day. It was a relief not to be around him and yet he still managed to distract me.

Ripples of guilt plagued me as I shared small talk with my friends at lunch. My frustration with him spiked when Mick mentioned something about his having to speak to the principal instead of being at lunch. It was just more evidence of how little he cared about the prestige of being at Oak Brook Academy.

On my way to my last class, Candy followed after me.

"Apple, are you okay?"

"I'm fine, why?" I quickened my pace to get to class on time.

"You just don't seem like yourself. I know that yesterday you said you didn't want to talk about it, but are you ready now?"

I stared into my friend's eyes. I wanted to tell her the truth. I wanted to ask for her help. But the truth was, I didn't know how. It embarrassed me to think that I had a crush on Ty.

"I'm fine, Candy, really. I'm just a little grumpy."

"If you say so." Candy pursed her lips.

"You're mad at me now, aren't you?" I frowned. "Don't be mad."

"I just don't know why you're hiding so much from me. It's

not like you. It's not like us. Don't you know how much I care about you?"

"I do." I smiled at her. "I do and I'm so grateful for it. But right now, I guess I need a little space to figure this all out. I promise, as soon as I get a handle on it, you'll be the first one I come to."

"I hope so." Candy stared at me. "Whatever it is, I'll find a way to help you."

"I know you always do." I gave her a brief hug. "But I really have to go to class. I've just got something on my mind and as soon as I'm ready to talk to someone about it, I'll let you know."

"Alright. I don't like it, but alright." Candy walked off down the hall.

I rounded the corner and nearly walked into Ty. He'd been standing so close to the corner that it struck me that he'd probably heard every word I'd just said. He stared at me, his eyes seeking deep into mine.

"Excuse me." I started to step around him.

He shifted in the same direction. "Apple."

"Excuse me, I said." I frowned as I observed the empty halls around us. I didn't want to be alone with him. I wasn't afraid of him, but I didn't like the flutter I felt deep within me every time I saw him. My words tangled in my mouth and I didn't know whether to yell at him or apologize to him.

"Just trying to get out of your way." He scowled at me as he shifted in the other direction, then continued past me and around the corner.

I turned toward him and opened my mouth to say something, but anger silenced me. He didn't have to be so rude every time I saw him. It was probably for the best that I didn't speak to him at all.

Throughout my last class, I thought about whether he would show up for the art club. After the way he'd spoken to me, I guessed that he wouldn't. But a part of me still hoped that he would. I told myself it was for Patrick's sake, since he enjoyed Ty so much. But I didn't think we would be able to work together. We couldn't even bump into each other in the hallway without having a problem. How could we get through almost two hours of art club?

After class, I took my time walking toward the bus stop. Maybe he would ask to join me. Maybe he would at least give me an idea of whether he would show up or not.

But of course, he didn't show up. In fact, I didn't see him at all. Not in the courtyard, not buzzing past on his skateboard —nowhere.

As I reached the bus stop, I decided that it was for the best. I couldn't concentrate around him and clearly he couldn't stand to be anywhere near me.

The bus arrived and the doors swung open. I stepped up onto the bus and paid, then froze when I heard someone behind me. A quick glance over my shoulder revealed Ty, his eyes locked to the windshield instead of me as he waited to board.

"Ty."

"Take your seat please, miss." The driver gestured toward the rear of the bus.

"Yes, I will. Just one second." I turned back to Ty. "I'm not sure that it's a good idea for you to participate—"

"No, don't." He suddenly met my eyes, his voice low but determined. "You're not going to do that."

"Ty, be reasonable." My heart raced as he continued to stare into my eyes.

"Time to go." The driver closed the doors and shifted the bus into drive. As we pulled away from the curb, the bus lurched and I stumbled forward at the edge of the steps.

Just before I would have fallen, I reached out and caught myself on Ty's shoulder.

His other hand landed on the curve of my side in an attempt to steady me. For an instant our eyes met and I felt my pounding heart skip a full beat.

Why?

"You should sit down." He let his hand fall away. His palm drifted along my side and coasted across my hip.

As I realized that my hand still rested on his shoulder, I took a step back and sat down in the first available seat.

Ty stood at the front of the bus and surveyed his options. More crowded than usual, there weren't many seats available.

I slid over in my seat and sighed. "Ty, just sit here."

"I'm not sure I should participate in that." He shot me an annoyed look.

"Just sit down." I grabbed him by the wrist and tugged him down into the seat beside me.

The moment he sat down I turned quickly to look out the window. Could he tell that my cheeks were hot?

"Thanks." He muttered the word. It could have been a curse, by the way he'd said it.

I bit into my bottom lip as tension flowed between us. Mrs. Ruby would expect me to keep Ty on as a volunteer and I needed him in order to add more kids to the club. If we were going to be stuck together, we had to at least be able to speak to each other. I tried to think of a way to open up a conversation.

As I shot down a few options in my head, Ty shifted closer to me.

"So, what's weighing on your mind?"

When I looked over at him, his gaze met mine.

"Huh?"

"I heard what you said to Candy in the hallway." He lowered his voice but continued to stare at me.

"You mean you spied on me." I stared back at him. "You were listening, weren't you? You had no reason to be there."

"Not everyone is out to get you, you know." He shook his head. "I had to get something from my locker."

"Okay." I frowned as I felt even more foolish. Was he right? Was I just being paranoid?

"So, what's bothering you?" He glanced at the road ahead of us, then looked back at me. "We've got some time, and like you said, I'm a good listener."

I couldn't help but smile at his words. "I didn't exactly say that."

"I am." He shrugged. "It's just a fact. Try me out."

"Why do you care?" I slid a little closer to the window. It seemed that every bump the bus hit caused him to scoot toward me.

"Let's see, we have to work together and you seem to have this unreasonable hatred of me. I thought maybe you just don't like skaters, then I overheard you talking in the hall. So maybe the reason you're being so hateful is because something is bothering you. If that's the case, then there's still a chance we could be friends. Isn't there?"

"You want to be my friend?" I watched as he slid his hands along the material of his jeans. Was he nervous?

TWELVE

"I want to be in the same room with you without either of us trying to bite the other's head off. That's all I'm asking." He frowned. "We're never going to like each other much—I get that —but that shouldn't mean we can't find a way to work together."

"Right."

I couldn't deny feeling a little crushed in response to his words. He was right, of course. We had nothing in common— there wasn't much chance that we could get along—but if we both made an effort, we might be able to get through a couple hours together.

"Let's give it our best shot." I turned my attention back to the window.

Although I wanted to know more about him—I was certainly curious—I decided it might be better not to dig. What I knew of him already was enough to make it clear that we didn't have anything in common. Why make it worse?

As we stepped off the bus, I felt some of the tension ease between us. But it was still there—in the way he looked at me out of the corner of his eye, shadowed by his hoodie.

And also in the way I avoided his touch when he opened the

door to the classroom for me. It was simple, all I had to be was nice or at the very least polite. I had done that plenty of times with people. I should be able to do it with Ty.

But as I stepped past him into the classroom and my elbow brushed across his stomach, a shiver raced up my spine. It was not a shiver of disgust, though I wanted to pretend that it was. It was a shiver of something far more pleasant. I closed my eyes and held my breath until it passed.

"You okay?"

I opened my eyes to his smile.

"Fine." I forced a smile in return.

"You looked like you were holding your breath. Do I smell or something?" He picked up the collar of his shirt and took a sniff.

"Your cologne *is* a bit strong." I shrugged and walked quickly up to the desk.

"Is it?" He sniffed his shirt again.

I did my best to ignore him. What was I supposed to say? Being near you makes me swoon? I didn't think that would go over too well.

Be polite, Apple, be polite. I sighed and tried to think of a way to smooth over my comment.

"It doesn't smell bad." The words hung awkwardly in the otherwise quiet room.

"No?" He glanced over at me as he pulled some paints out of the storage closet. "You like it?"

"No, not at all." I frowned.

"So it does smell bad?" He raised an eyebrow.

"No, that's not what I meant." I sighed. "I mean, it smells fine. But it doesn't matter whether or not I like it, does it?"

"I guess not..." He stared at me for a long moment. As he started to speak again, a stream of kids burst into the room.

Relieved for the distraction, I turned my attention to them

and soon forgot about my awkward moment. I had plenty of them, but around Ty, they seemed far worse.

Once I had the kids settled with an activity, I noticed that Ty and Patrick were working together on a new project.

"I thought you might like to try some different textures on wood." Ty leaned a large piece of plywood against a wall. "It's interesting to see how the paint reacts to the wood."

"Okay, I guess." Patrick shrugged, then smiled. "Do I get to throw things?"

"Sure. Pick your weapon." Ty grinned.

I walked over to them and looked at the wood. "Where did you get that from? It wasn't in the storage closet."

"I picked it up yesterday and dropped it off at the school." He shrugged. "I thought he might like it."

"You thought right." I smiled as I watched Patrick attack the piece of wood. A few of the other kids walked over, curious as well. I braced myself for the potential meltdown. "But it's hard to let one kid do something different without the others getting upset."

"It's okay." Patrick looked over at the other kids. "Want to try?" He held up a sponge soaked in paint.

Stunned, I watched as Patrick and a few other children began to interact together with no issue. Patrick didn't have any friends that I knew of and seeing him laugh and instruct the other kids revealed a side to him that I didn't even know existed.

"Wow." I looked over at Ty. "Do you see what you did here?"

"I didn't bring enough wood for everyone." Ty frowned. "I'm sorry. It was a stupid idea."

"No, it wasn't." I stepped closer to him, and without thinking it through, placed my hand against his cheek. "Look." I turned his face toward the kids interacting. "That is what you did. Just your presence here has totally transformed Patrick."

"I didn't do that." He ducked his head away from my touch and swallowed hard. "Patrick didn't transform. That's who he really is. I just gave him the space to show it off."

"However you want to put it, it's given him an entirely different experience." I tucked my hands into my pockets as my cheeks grew hot. What was I thinking? Why had I touched him that way? It obviously made him uncomfortable. "I should check on the other kids."

"Sure." He nodded and kept his gaze on Patrick and his new friends.

I walked among the easels, observing each of the creations and offering praise as well as gentle instruction. But my eyes kept gravitating back in Ty's direction.

There was definitely a lot more to him—hidden beneath that hoodie. Maybe it wasn't all good, but I doubted that it was all bad either. He had a heart for kids like I did and in particular for kids that others might overlook. It made me wonder if that had something to do with the chip on his shoulder. Had he found a kindred spirit in Patrick?

I didn't realize how long I'd been staring until he turned toward me and boldly met my eyes.

"You still don't trust me with the kids?" He crossed his arms.

Startled, I tried to think of the right thing to say. I couldn't tell him that I'd been thinking about how he was probably a troubled soul that needed the same kind of tenderness that he showed Patrick. But I also didn't want him to think that I didn't like him working with the kids.

"It's not that."

"No?" He glanced at the kids again, then walked over to me. "Then what is it? I'm not sure that I like being watched all the time."

Again, I had to bite back my confession. "I wasn't watching you. I was just curious about some things."

"Like what?"

"Like how you're so good with kids. Do you have any brothers or sisters?" My heart pounded. Yes, changing the subject would be a good cover.

"No. It's just me. But I used to take care of a lot of the kids in my neighborhood. Well, you could say we were all one pack." His expression softened.

"That sounds nice." I smiled as I wondered what memory he might be reliving. "I don't have any brothers or sisters either, but I didn't have too many neighborhood kids to hang around with." I didn't mention the towering security gates or the fact that I had a bodyguard who traveled with me everywhere. My mother went through an intense helicopter phase.

"That explains it, I guess." He crossed his arms as he studied me.

"Explains what?"

"Your awkwardness—I mean, that you don't like to talk to people—how shy you are." He frowned. "That didn't come out quite right."

"No, it's fine." I forced down the hurt that I felt. "I am awkward. Everyone knows it. It doesn't matter. I should start cleaning up." I busied myself collecting paints and tried to ignore the ache in my chest.

Ty wasn't wrong. I was awkward. But he'd made it clear that he noticed, and that left me more than a little mortified. If only I didn't care what he thought, I might have been able to let it roll off my back.

But I did care. I cared way too much.

THIRTEEN

The bus ride home was even more awkward. Ty and I sat next to each other, but I did my best to remain as far from him as possible. When we stepped off the bus, he turned to look at me.

"Do you want me to walk you to your dorm?"

"Why?" I stared at him.

"Uh, no reason I guess. See you tomorrow?"

"Right. Remember we have that trip tomorrow." I winced as I recalled the way he'd spoken about Mrs. Ruby. Why did it have to be him that I had a crush on?

"Sure, I'll be there." He nodded to me, then turned and walked off in the other direction, away from the school.

I started to warn him that he shouldn't be wandering off of school grounds but thought better of it. He was old enough to know better. He could take his own chances. If he wanted to get into more trouble, that was his business. Still, I wondered where he was going and why.

In an attempt to distract myself from those questions I hurried through the courtyard and toward the dormitories. I could pick up a good book, turn on some loud music, and completely forget about Ty. All I had to do was try.

I stepped into my dorm room and found it empty. At least I would have a few minutes of peace to sort through my thoughts.

I'd just put on my headphones and picked up my book when there was a loud knock followed by Maby's laughter.

"Come on in. The door's unlocked."

Maby stumbled in with several packages in her arms.

"Let me help you!" I jumped up just in time to save one of the packages. "What's all this?"

"From Mom." She grinned as she stacked them up on the kitchen counter. "She took a trip to France. I'm sure she bought something in every store she stopped in."

"Wow!" I smiled. "That's wonderful."

"I guess." Maby looked over the packages. "Sometimes I wonder if it's a bit much."

"What's a bit much?" Candy walked into the room.

"My mom." Maby pointed to the packages.

"She loves you." I thought of my own mother. She often showered me with gifts. Although I didn't need half the things she bought me, it was our ritual and it made us both happy. "I'm sure she would have rather been shopping with you."

"Ah, me too." Maby shook her head. "Anyway, I have to run to a meeting, can I leave these here for now?"

"Sure, no problem."

After Maby left, Candy looked straight into my eyes. "What's wrong?"

"What do you mean?"

"Apple! I can see it in your eyes. You're stressed. What is going on?"

"Nothing, nothing at all. You should open your packages. I'm going to take my book into my room." I snatched it up from the sofa and headed straight for my room.

"Apple!" She followed after me and pushed open my door before I could get it closed. "What's going on here?"

"It's not a big deal. I just want some time alone, alright?" I sat down on my bed and did my best to appear calm, but my heart continued to slam against my chest. What if I told her the truth? Would she laugh at me?

"That's enough." She pushed the door to my room closed and strode across the carpet toward me. "You're going to tell me exactly what's going on now."

"Ugh." I flopped back on my bed and closed my eyes. "I'm not sure that I can. I don't even know how to explain it to myself."

"Don't try to make sense out of it, just tell me what's going on with you." She sat down on the end of my bed. "You know we always talk everything out. Don't let this pin you down. Once you talk about it, everything will be more clear."

"Maybe that's what I'm afraid of the most." I sat up again and looked into her eyes. "I've gotten myself into a real mess, Candy—one that I never expected."

"Hey, things happen." She patted the back of my hand. "Whatever it is, I'm sure we can figure it out. But you have to tell me first."

"It's Ty." I forced his name from between my lips. Even just saying it was enough to send my heart racing. Why? I frowned. "I hate to admit it, but it's Ty."

"What do you mean it's Ty?" She narrowed her eyes. "Has he done something to hurt you? If so, I will sic Mick, Chuckles, and Wes on him. Just tell me what he did to you."

"He didn't do anything to me. I mean, not exactly." I frowned. "He didn't hurt me or do anything wrong. It's just I..." I took a breath. "I don't know how to explain it."

"Oh my goodness!" Candy jumped up from the bed and gasped. "Does my little Apple have her first crush?"

"It's not my first one, I've had crushes before." I clapped my hand over my mouth and winced.

"You do!" Candy squealed, then jumped up and down with excitement. "I can't wait to tell Maby!"

"No!" I jumped off the end of the bed and landed right in front of Candy. "You can't tell her, not ever. Promise me!" I stared hard into her eyes.

"What? Why not?" Candy frowned. "She'd be so hurt if you didn't tell her."

"Candy, if Maby finds out, Mick will find out eventually and you know it. Then Mick will tell Ty and I will be even more humiliated than I already am! Please!" I grabbed her hand and looked into her eyes. "You can't tell anyone, please! Promise me?"

"Alright, I promise." She sighed. "But I think you're being ridiculous. Maby would keep it a secret."

"I'm sure she would, but Mick has ways of finding out everything." I felt some relief as I sat back down on the bed. "Besides, just you knowing is embarrassing enough for me. I want to be able to pretend that none of this ever happened. Unfortunately, I haven't figured out how to do that yet. That's why I need your help."

"I will help." She sat down beside me. "But first we need to figure out what kind of help you need."

"What do you mean? I just told you the kind of help I need. I need to get rid of this crush so I can go back to normal. I need to stop thinking about Ty every time I close my eyes."

"I'm not sure if that's the kind of help you need." She folded her legs and turned to look at me. "If you have these feelings for him, maybe the help you need is learning how to express them."

"No!" I shook my head. "Absolutely not. I don't have feelings for him. All I have is an annoying crush. I'm sure that it has something to do with everyone pairing up around here. I honestly hadn't even thought about Ty before. There's nothing real between us. I just happen to be feeling a little lonely, I guess."

"Or maybe getting to know Ty made you realize that he's a pretty interesting guy. Have you considered that?"

"Not exactly. But it wouldn't matter anyway. Even if he is interesting—even if there is more to him than I first thought—he has zero interest in me. So, what does it matter?"

"How can he have any interest in you if you never speak?" She snapped her fingers. "I've got it. I'm going to teach you a few things. Easy conversation starters. That way when you two see each other on the trip tomorrow, you can actually talk."

"I don't know." I frowned. "I guess it couldn't hurt to try."

"The easiest way to start a conversation is to ask about music. Everyone loves music. So, you ask about what kind of music he likes or maybe if he's listened to anything new lately. Then you share what kind of music you like." She brushed her palms against each other. "Easy as pie."

"Okay, I think I could do that." I nodded.

"Next, you can ask him about something you know he's interested in, like football or skateboards."

"But I don't know anything about either of those things." I sighed.

"You don't have to know, trust me. If he's into it, he'll explain everything to you. It's a good way to spark a conversation if you get stuck."

"Thanks, Candy. I just really hope we can find a way to be friends. You should see him with the kids at art club. I've never seen anyone so natural with them."

"Oh?" Candy smiled. She leaned closer to me and looked into my eyes. "I think the first thing you should do is figure out if you really want to be *just friends*."

"Of course. That's the only option." I shrugged.

"All I'm saying is that you should think about it." She gave me a warm hug. "I promise not to pressure you. But maybe you two would be really good together."

"Not a chance." I narrowed my eyes.

My stomach flipped. And my heart beat faster. Was there a chance?

FOURTEEN

The question lingered in my mind all night. It woke me up a few times and made it quite difficult for me to fall asleep again. Was there a chance with me and Ty?

I wanted to be excited about the trip the next day. I wanted to look forward to exploring works of art. I wanted to be curious about Mrs. Ruby's surprise. Instead, all I felt was nervous. Nervous that I'd have to talk to Ty. Nervous that he'd want to talk to me. Nervous that he wouldn't. I couldn't figure out what I was more nervous about.

As I arrived at class the next morning, I thought twice about going in. Maybe if I turned around and went back to bed, the whole day would disappear and I wouldn't have to deal with any of it.

Instead, I forced myself to step through the door. If I just didn't show up, that would only cause more attention to be focused on me. I'd go and get through the day and then it would be over.

"No need to be dramatic, Apple."

"What's that?" Alana looked over at me. "Are you talking to yourself again?"

79

"Maybe." I cringed. Then I grabbed her hand. "Will you be my partner today?"

"Sure." She smiled. "I think we're going to have fun."

"Great." I squeezed her hand, then released it.

As long as I was partnered up with Alana I could easily get through the day. Although I had rehearsed a few of Candy's conversation starters in the mirror, I wasn't sure that I'd ever be able to actually use them.

"Everyone!" Mrs. Ruby clapped her hands together. "Listen up! We're going to have a great trip. But in order to make that happen, we all need to pay attention, stick together, and cooperate!" She swept her gaze over the gathered students, then sighed. "Does anyone know where Ty is?"

"I'm here!" Ty rushed through the door. "Sorry, Mrs. Ruby, I—"

"Nope, no time for excuses." She waved her clipboard at him. "You're the first in line. Everyone line up behind Ty and we're all going to walk out to the van together. It'll be a little cramped in there, but I think we'll be fine."

I lined up behind Alana and did my best not to think about where Ty had been and why he might have been late. That lasted for about thirty seconds. Halfway down the hall, he glanced back at me and I met his eyes.

An electric jolt ran through me. Why was he always so late? Why did he look at me like that? Why couldn't I look away from him?

"Everyone in the van! Hurry! We are running behind!" Mrs. Ruby shooed us all onto the van with a swish of her clipboard through the air.

As I settled into the seat next to Alana, I calmed down some. From his seat all the way in the back of the van, Ty likely couldn't even see me. I didn't have to worry about him catching my eye. In fact, packed into the van, I doubted there would be any chance for conversation.

"Mick and I have been looking for a new place to eat." Alana chattered beside me. "I'm hoping to scope out the cafe in this museum and see what we might like."

"Wait, what?" I looked over at her. "You know where we're going?"

"Sure, it's this amazing museum with a giant spiral staircase. Not too many people know about it, that's why I suggested it to Mrs. Ruby. There are some great pieces to see. Plus the staircase is really cool." She grinned.

"That sounds like fun." I began to relax. Yes, this trip still had a chance to be fun.

When we arrived at the museum, Mrs. Ruby hurried everyone off the van. As people began to pair up on the sidewalk Mrs. Ruby clapped her hands to get everyone's attention.

"Everyone will have a partner. I took the liberty of pairing you all up this morning." She began to call out names of partners. "Alana and Jesse."

"Jesse?" Alana peered at the boy. "I don't think we've ever said two words."

"Good luck." I frowned.

"I'm sorry, Apple, I'll see you later." Alana walked over to Jesse.

"Now everyone, I did my best to pair you together with people that you might not have a lot in common with, because I'm hoping that you can pick out a few paintings in the museum and compare your opinions on them. I always find that getting another person's point of view on art can totally change my perspective."

Although I actually liked her idea, I braced myself as I waited to see who she would pair me up with.

One by one my classmates were paired, until there were

very few left. Me, a few other classmates, and Ty. I shot him a brief look and found him looking straight at me.

No, no, no. I closed my eyes and held my breath. When I opened my eyes again, I saw a faint smile on his lips.

"Let's see." She looked over the list on her clipboard. "Ty, you're going to be with Apple. Oh, that works out perfectly, doesn't it? I'm sure the two of you have gotten to know each other at art club."

My heart sank. It would be impossible to avoid having to use my conversation starters if we had to spend the day together looking at art. I cringed at what he might have to say about my favorite paintings. What could he like? I doubted that he'd ever been to an art museum. Did he even have a preference?

"Great." Ty looked at me. "I mean, if you're okay with it."

"Sure, of course." What could I say? *The last thing I want to do is be alone with you. I'm pretty sure that melting into the ground would be better than anything I'm experiencing right now.*

No, those wouldn't be very good conversation starters. I tried to picture myself calm. Maybe if I could imagine it, I would become it.

As the class funneled into the museum, I hung back a few steps. As soon as I walked through the door, I would be faced with hours alone with Ty. My skin tingled from the tips of my toes to the top of my head. How would I survive?

"Let me get that." Ty reached behind me to grab the door. He held it open for Mrs. Ruby, who stepped inside. Then he looked at me. "Just you and me, huh?"

"I guess." I offered a nervous laugh.

"This should be interesting."

"Yup." I stared at him.

"So, are you going to go in?" He gestured to the open door.

"Oh right, I guess I should. That's what doors are for, right?"

My eyes widened with every word I spoke. How could I make it worse? I started through the door and caught the tip of my shoe on the tip of his. "Oops, sorry."

"It's fine." He smiled as he stepped in behind me.

"Are you sure? I mean, maybe you should sit down for a little while—make sure that I didn't break any toes."

"I'm sure." He took a few steps further into the museum, then stopped and looked up. "Wow!" He tipped his head all the way back. "Would you look at that?"

"It's amazing." I stepped up beside him.

"Race you to the top?" He grinned.

"Not a chance!" I gasped.

"I was just kidding." He laughed, then shook his head. "I'm sure there's plenty to see. We can take our time." He paused. "Unless you want to split up. I'm sure Mrs. Ruby will never know the difference."

"There you go wanting to break the rules again." I frowned.

"There you go, judging me again." He quirked an eyebrow. "I'm not the one that looks like she'd rather be anywhere else than with me right now. I'm just trying to be polite. It's up to you. I'm not going to force you to do anything that you don't want to do." He crossed his arms. "So, what's it going to be?"

I studied him for a long moment. It would be easier to go with his plan. We could split up. I could hide out. I could enjoy the art. But that spark that burned inside of me wouldn't let me turn and walk away.

"Okay. Let's just find a couple of pieces to compare opinions on. That's the assignment, right? Then we can go our separate ways." My heartbeat quickened as I looked at him. "Deal?"

FIFTEEN

"If that's what you want, Apple." Ty nodded as he slid his hands into his pockets. "Let's get started."

"Good." I managed to breathe easily again. We would spend a short time together and soon enough it would be over.

I followed his lead up the spiral staircase. When he paused on one of the steps, I followed his line of sight to the painting on the wall. The mixture of colors—deep reds, pale oranges, and vivid pinks—spoke to me as well. In the center of it all, feminine features splayed out in what looked like a mouth that was screaming.

"Do you like this one?" He glanced over at me.

"It's hard for me to find art that I don't like." I studied the lines in the painting. "But this one—it just seems a little over-done. It seems like the artist was trying too hard to capture the essence of joy."

"Joy?" He stared at me. "Is that what you see?"

"Sure. All the colors are bright and the paint strokes are wide. The woman seems to be crying out in celebration." I looked back at him. "Why, what do you see?"

"I see agony." He grabbed the railing of the staircase and leaned forward some. "I see a woman exploding."

"Really?" I took a step back and looked at the painting again. As I tilted my head to the side and shifted a bit, I felt my shoulder bump up against Ty's. I expected him to move, but instead, he remained perfectly still. I shifted away and narrowed my eyes. "I guess I can see that too. Isn't it interesting that we can look at the same painting and see something so different?"

"It doesn't surprise me." He continued up the steps.

"It doesn't?" I followed after him. "Why not?"

"Life is different through different eyes."

"So, which of us do you think is right?" I continued up the spiral stairs, only a step or two behind him.

"Neither." He glanced back over his shoulder.

"Neither?" I stared up at him. "One of us has to be at least close. Hold on, I'll look up the artist on my phone and see what was written about the painting."

"Don't bother." He placed his hand over my phone and looked into my eyes. "It doesn't matter what the author painted or why. The only thing that matters is how we see it."

"I guess you're right." I tucked my phone back into my pocket. "I've never thought about it that way."

"Of course you haven't." He reached the next level of paintings and paused. "What about this one?" He gestured to a painting full of geometrical shapes that were just off-kilter enough to be imperfect and all painted a dark blue shade.

"Wait, what do you mean by of course I haven't?" I stepped up beside him.

"Aren't we supposed to be looking at paintings?" He remained focused on the art in front of him.

"I'm just asking what you meant."

"I just meant that sometimes people don't think outside the

box unless they're forced to." He turned to face me. "You don't seem like the kind of person that has ever been forced into anything."

"Oh, that spoiled rich girl tune again?" I leaned against the railing beside him. "Do you ever get tired of that one?"

"That's not what I meant." He frowned. "Let's just get this done." He tipped his head toward the painting. "What do you think?"

"I think it's pretty bland. I don't really understand what people get out of this type of art. It makes me feel cold." I wrapped my arms around myself.

"Me too—a little." He moved closer to me. "Do you see the tiny triangles?"

"Tiny triangles?" I tried not to notice how close he was to me. Then he leaned even closer as he pointed out the small triangles that created the outline of several of the shapes.

"How interesting." My eyes widened. "I didn't even notice those before. Thanks for showing me. That opens up an entirely different idea of what this artist might have been painting."

"It just looks like shapes to me. What more do you see?" He crossed his arms on top of the railing.

I could feel the warmth of his elbow against the sleeve of my shirt. I closed my eyes for just a second, then opened them again.

"Layers. As if on the surface, we must present one thing, but underneath we are completely different. The cold, sharp lines lack emotion. It feels as if there is isolation from anything of meaning." I sighed, then straightened up. "Not sure if that makes any sense."

"It makes a lot of sense." His eyes settled on mine. "You really do love art, don't you?"

"I do." I smiled. "When I paint, it feels as if I'm in an

entirely different universe and sometimes that's exactly where I want to be. Most of the time, actually." I leaned forward and the angled cut of my hair sloped across my face.

"You always want to hide." He murmured his words, just before his silky fingertips caught my hair and brushed it back along my cheek. "Why is that?"

My heart lurched in reaction to his touch, then it beat swiftly as his question hung in the air between us.

"I don't hide," I whispered.

"You do," he whispered back and tucked my hair behind my ear. "Why?"

"We should keep moving, we have one more painting to do." I brushed past him and continued up the stairs. My cheek still tingled where he'd touched it. How did he know how to cut through all my defenses without my even noticing the attempt?

As I reached the top of the spiral staircase, a large painting that hung from the high ceiling stopped me in my tracks.

"Interesting." He paused beside me and stared at the painting. "I don't think I've ever seen anything quite like this. Have you?"

"No." I watched as the painting fluttered. Although it appeared to be one solid canvas, it was actually several different slivers. With the slightest breeze, it fluttered and the painting changed.

"Wow." He shook his head. "That's crazy."

"It's beautiful." I saw my own emotions reflected in the movement of the painting. One minute, I was solid, the next I was in pieces as I tried to make sense of the way that Ty made me feel.

"I think it has an interesting pattern. But I'm not sure I like the choppiness of it. I mean, could you even call it one painting or is it just a bunch of little ones?" He squinted at the painting. "I like the concept, though."

"We're all a million pieces." I tipped my head to the side. "That's the meaning I get from it."

"Are you?" He gazed at me from beneath strands of his long blond hair.

Before I could hesitate, my fingertips swept through those locks, brushing them away from his eyes so that he could see better.

"Sometimes." I let my hand settle back on the curve of the railing. "Aren't you?"

"Just one." He lowered his eyes and all of the hair I'd moved out of the way fell right back into place.

"Really? Don't you ever feel like you're falling apart?" I shifted closer to him as a pair of students continued past us onto the top floor of the museum.

"I feel like I'm the only one I have to hold onto, so I hold tight. I don't want to lose any pieces." He smiled. "I used to flutter, just like that." He pointed to the painting. "Then I figured out who I was and everything fit back together."

"It's that simple, huh?" I grinned in an attempt to hide my jealousy. I had no idea who I was. How had he figured out so much at such a young age?

"It can be. I think." He grabbed my hand and pulled me off of the steps onto the top floor. "Come with me. I want to show you something."

"How can you have anything to show me? You've never been here before." I thought about pulling my hand away, but just for a moment I decided to enjoy it. It didn't do any harm to savor the feeling of his hand curled around mine or the excitement of his wanting to show something to me. Did it?

My heart skipped a beat as he pulled me through a door along a hallway.

"I might have been here before." He glanced over his shoulder at me as the door fell shut behind us.

Suddenly, darkness surrounded us. I took a sharp breath and reached for the doorknob. When I tried to turn it, the knob only twisted so far before it stopped. "We're locked in!"

SIXTEEN

"Breathe." His hands settled on my shoulders.

I could feel the warmth of his touch and the pressure of it, but I could barely see him.

"I don't want to breathe! Ty, what is this? We need to get out of here!" I reached up and wrapped my hands around his, just to be certain that he was there.

"Relax. You're invisible. We both are." He murmured his words.

"What?" My heartbeat quickened as I became more and more aware of being alone with him. My thoughts spun so swiftly through my mind that I couldn't manage to hold onto a single one.

"Apple, it's an exhibit." He stepped closer to me.

My eyes adjusted to the darkness enough that I could see the fine details of his face and a hint of his light blue eyes.

"What are you talking about?"

"It's meant to immerse you in the sensation of being invisible. The walls, floor, and ceiling are all designed to bend distance, to create a sense of eternity. Can you feel it?" His lips spread into a smile.

"You could have warned me." My heart slowed just a little, but the continued presence of his touch left me just as flustered as the piece of art we'd just discussed.

"That ruins the effect." He drew his hands away from my shoulders. "I thought you would like it—since you spend so much time trying to avoid interaction."

"I do not." I frowned. Then I sighed. "Alright, but not all the time."

"It's nothing to be ashamed of, Apple." He lingered close to me, but we were no longer touching. "I find it pretty peaceful actually. Don't you?"

Not with you here.

I managed to keep that thought to myself. I closed my eyes. I held my breath. I couldn't think of him that way. I just couldn't.

"Breathe." His voice drifted right beside my ear, sending a shiver up my spine. "You have to breathe, Apple."

Was that warmth on my cheek his breath? Were his fingertips hovering as close to my wrist as I thought they were? I opened my eyes and took a breath.

"That's better." He smiled.

I could see it through the darkness as well as the gleam of his eyes. Something about the dim lighting helped me to relax, despite the fact that he was just as close.

"It is pretty peaceful."

"You're free now." He met my eyes.

"It does feel freeing." I smiled at the thought.

"I meant, you're free now. We did what we agreed to do." He tilted his head toward the other side of the room. "The door out is over here. I can show you the way."

"Oh." My heart pounded. "Maybe we could stay here just a little longer."

"I'd like to." He took a deep breath. I noticed a droop in his shoulders as he relaxed.

"I think I'm not the only one that likes to hide." I shifted just a little closer to him, but in the process, my little finger brushed against his. "Is that why you're always getting into trouble?"

"Not always." He murmured his response. His little finger glided back against mine.

Was that just him shifting his weight or did he mean to touch me? My heart began to race. Alone, in the dark with Ty. What was I thinking?

"We should go." I brushed past him and toward the door.

"Wait." He caught my hand just as I stepped away. "You have to be careful. There are things you can bump into."

"I'll be fine." I pulled my hand away as a wave of dizziness rushed over me. Were those actual butterflies in my stomach? I felt my way forward through a few cushions and what felt like pieces of furniture. Whoever had created this exhibit didn't consider safety a priority.

"Here." His arm landed on my shoulders and curled around before I could step aside. "This way." He guided me through the remainder of the room, then opened a door that I hadn't noticed before.

As soon as the light flooded in, I realized my mistake. My cheeks were hotter than I'd ever felt them. Would he notice?

I ducked my head and stepped quickly through the door. Once out in the bright light, I had to squint in order to see.

"Wow, that was an interesting experience." I blinked in an attempt to regain my vision.

"Give yourself a second to adjust." His arm lingered around my shoulder.

"Thanks." I pulled away and took a sharp breath. "For your help in there. And for showing it to me." I met his eyes. "I really like music. Do you?"

He stared at me with a raised eyebrow.

"I mean, what kind of music do you like? If you listen to

music, that is. Everyone does. Right?" My voice broke as I laughed around my words.

"Uh, I mostly listen to classical while I work and otherwise rock—a little bit of rap here and there." He shrugged.

"While you work?" I scrunched up my nose. "You don't expect me to believe that you have a job, do you? You would always be late!"

"Ah, I see." He rubbed the back of his neck. "Maybe it's best we go our own way now."

"Ugh, I'm sorry, that came out the wrong way." I sank down on a nearby bench. "I honestly don't mean to be insulting, Ty. I just have a hard time talking to people until I get comfortable around them."

"Well, what's it going to take for you to get comfortable around me?" He sat down beside me.

"I'm not sure." I bit into my bottom lip.

I had a few ideas. He could stop being so attractive. He could stop making my heart race just by looking at me. He could definitely stop touching me.

"It just takes time." I stared down at my hands. "I'm sorry, I know it's weird. I really would like to be your friend."

"Don't be sorry." He placed his hand over mine. His voice softened. "I've got time."

I looked up at him and immediately regretted it. There he was with those bright blue eyes and that sweet smile. How did he manage to make my mind spin every time he looked at me? His fingertips stroked across the back of my hand in a slow circle with just enough pressure to remind me they were there.

"Ty, I should—uh." My words caught in my throat as he looked into my eyes.

"You should what?" He leaned closer to me.

"I just think..." I tried again, but my voice trailed off breathlessly.

"Apple." He lowered his voice to a whisper as his lips hovered beside my ear. "Breathe."

"Football!" I blurted the word out and jumped up from the bench in the same moment. The movement was so sudden that I jerked my hand out of his and he banged his wrist on the bench.

"What?" He stared at me his eyes wide.

"Football. Do you want to talk about football?" I stood at a safe distance as I looked at him. I sucked down air in an attempt to calm myself.

"No. Not really." He smiled as he gazed at me. "I'd rather talk about you."

SEVENTEEN

"Probably not the best idea." I frowned. "We have to go soon."

"We have the van ride back to school." He stood up and walked over to me. "You said it takes time, right? So, we'll have to spend some time together. I want things to be good between us. I want to stick around at art club."

Art club, I reminded myself. That was why he was interested. He wanted to get his community service hours filled and he wanted to be around the kids. It didn't have much to do with me.

"I want you to stick around. The kids do." I cleared my throat. "It's been great having you there."

"You mean when we're not fighting with each other." He smiled and shrugged. "That's what I'd like to prevent."

"Me too. I can't stand it." I sighed. Then I noticed his frown. "Not you. I didn't mean that I can't stand you, just what you say. No, I mean—what I say—what we say to each other." I groaned.

"Relax." He shook his head. "We're not going to get anywhere if you get nervous over everything you say."

"You're right. Oh." I glanced at my watch again. "I told Mrs.

Ruby I'd meet her downstairs. I'd better go. See you in the van."
I turned and headed down the spiral steps.

As I moved quickly down them, I could feel his gaze on me.
He could watch me the whole way down. What if I slipped?
How embarrassing would that be? I slowed myself down and
tried to appear calm and collected as I reached the last step.

No, I didn't just run away from someone who'd suggested
he'd like to talk more about me. I didn't make up a lame excuse
that he likely didn't believe just to escape.

"Apple! Where's your partner?" Mrs. Ruby walked over to
me. "Did he leave you alone? I'll have to speak to him about
that."

"No, Mrs. Ruby, he didn't leave me alone. We finished our
assignment and I thought I'd see if you needed help with
anything." I glanced around at the scattered students. "Maybe
gathering everyone up?"

"Yes, that would be great, thank you. We do need to get on
the road." She smiled as she glanced around at the works of art
that surrounded her. "Isn't it wonderful here?"

"Yes, it is." I smiled in return.

Once I'd herded everyone toward the van, I began to search
for Ty. Finally, I spotted him already in the van seated in the
back. If I'd wanted to, I could have boarded and sat down
beside him.

Instead, I focused on getting the other students on. This
created a buffer between us and made it impossible for me to sit
beside him. Then again, maybe he didn't want to sit beside me,
maybe that was why he was the first one in the van.

The entire drive back to the school I over-analyzed the
possibilities. When we were alone in the darkness, I could have
sworn he'd made an effort to touch me. I thought his arm
around me meant that he might be interested. But, now that I
was in the light again, I could clearly see that he'd just been

being nice. He wanted to be my friend so he could keep attending the art club.

The first moment I could, I got out of the van and headed straight for my sacred space. I didn't want to take the chance of running into Ty again—not until I got some things straightened out in my mind.

As I wove my way through buildings in the direction of one in particular, I checked over my shoulder to be sure that no one had followed me. I needed some time to myself. I needed a way to express what I was feeling. For me, there was only one way to do that.

When I reached the abandoned building, I was relieved to see that there was no sign of anyone else inside. I shared the space with my closest friends, but much of the time I had it to myself.

I pushed open the door and stepped inside. Once I'd confirmed it was empty, I gathered up my paints. It was time to get it all out—the best way I knew how. The interior of the building had become a paradise for me. I could paint on any wall, even on the ceiling.

I chose a space not far from the window, right beside the pile of cushions that covered the floor. I grabbed my paints and began to spill my feelings out onto the wall. Normally it would be a landscape of some kind. Many times, I painted images of the sky. But as the lines and curves began to take shape on the wall in front of me, my heart dropped.

This wasn't my usual creation. Not at all.

Instead, it was a face. As the details began to fill in, they confirmed my first guess.

"Ty." I stared at the image I'd created. How could I paint him?

Annoyed, I grabbed a thick paintbrush and painted over the image until no trace of it remained.

After a few deep breaths, I tried again. I'd just finished outlining his face and hair again when I heard noise behind me. I glanced over my shoulder to see Alana and Mick land on the pillows on the floor.

"Uh, excuse me?" I stared down at them, my paintbrush still in my hand, and did my very best not to sneer at them.

"Oops." Alana laughed as she rolled off Mick. "Sorry, Apple, I didn't know you were here."

"Me either." Mick jumped to his feet. "I guess we were a little distracted."

"Seems that way." I rolled my eyes and turned back to the image I'd just painted on the wall.

"Who is that?" Alana peered at the painting in progress.

"No one." I slashed some blue paint over Ty's golden hair. I couldn't let anyone find out, especially not Mick. He would never let me live it down. "I'm done here. You guys can have some time alone." I pushed past Alana, toward the door.

"Apple, is everything okay?" Alana caught my hand and looked into my eyes.

"Great." I smiled at her, then pulled away. "Enjoy." I hurried to the door as my heart raced.

If I stayed a moment longer, I was certain that they would figure out who I'd been painting. How would I explain that to them? I couldn't even explain it to myself.

As the door closed behind me, I wondered where to go now. If I didn't find some place to hide away, I ran the risk of seeing Ty again. Although the thought caused a jolt of excitement within me, I also had no idea what I would say to him. It would be safer if I was back in my dorm, hidden away from everyone, just like I liked it.

After one glance over my shoulder in the direction of the hideout I'd just left, I broke into a light jog.

Yes, young love was very much in bloom at Oak Brook Academy. I knew it happened. It had happened to Mick and Alana, it had happened to Fi and Wes, but that didn't mean that it could happen for me.

EIGHTEEN

I was almost to the dorms when I heard the grind and roll of wheels against the sidewalk. My heart skipped a beat at the sound.

Yes, of course it was Ty. There weren't many other skaters around.

It was too late to run away, unless I wanted to be completely rude.

"There you are. I was looking for you." He walked up to me and smiled. "I thought maybe you were avoiding me."

"No, not at all, just busy." I continued toward the dorms.

"Busy with what? There's no art club this afternoon." He matched his pace with mine.

Busy with anything that doesn't involve you.

I clenched my teeth and tried to resist saying another word.

Ty stepped in front of me. "Apple?"

"Ty." I took a step back.

"Stop." He caught my elbow with a gentle grasp. "If we're going to make this work, you've got to stop doing that."

"Doing what?" My heart pounded as his fingers continued to clutch my elbow.

"Hiding. Taking off on me." He shook his head. "I thought we were making some real progress at the museum. I thought..." He paused, then released my elbow. "I don't know what I thought."

"Look, I'm awkward. I'm always going to be awkward. There's not much I can do about that." I shrugged. "It's just how I am."

"It's not just that." He caught my hand again as I turned away. "What's this?" He turned my hand in his own. "Blue paint?"

"Yes, that's what it is." I bit into my bottom lip as I recalled painting his face, not once, but twice on the wall. What if he found out about that? He'd probably think I was some kind of stalker. I already thought I might be turning into one.

"Have you been painting?" He tapped his fingertip against some of the paint. "Oh, yup, fresh."

"Yes, I was painting."

He looked past me in the direction I'd come from. "Where?"

"Just around. I have to go. See you later." I turned and walked away.

This time, he didn't stop me. I had to admit I was a little disappointed, but also relieved to make an official escape. If I could avoid him for the entire weekend, I wouldn't have to see him until Monday. Surely in that amount of time I would be able to shake him from my mind.

I knew it bothered him that I didn't want to speak with him, but it was something that he would just have to endure for the moment. I needed my head clear, and if that meant steering clear of him, then that was what I would do.

Friday night was easy. He had a football game and I had zero interest in attending. Instead, I focused on some studies I had slipped behind in.

I worked hard to keep my grades up. I didn't want to be a

student who only attended because their parents forked over enough money. Yes, my parents had more than enough money for the tuition, but I wanted to take advantage of the education that afforded me.

Unfortunately, I just wasn't great with academics. The amount of time I put into my homework and studying for tests was at least twice the time that Candy spent and she still scored higher on tests. No matter what I did, my mind tended to be a blur.

That night, it was even worse, thanks to Ty. He played a huge role in distracting me from anything academic.

In my imagination, he came up to me, threw his arms around me, and pulled me close for a kiss. In my imagination, he declared his love for me and told me that he wanted no one but me. In my imagination, I loved every minute of it.

But in reality, I knew the story would be much different. Even though I'd finally admitted to having a crush on him—at least to myself—that didn't mean he had feelings for me.

He'd made enough comments about me to surmise that he thought of me as a spoiled rich girl without much that held his attention. His attempts at friendship—I knew—came from a place of self-preservation. I could see the two of us being friends, but even that would be awkward, because I didn't think being friends would be enough for me.

I'd never felt this way about anyone before, and at this point, I hoped that I would never feel this way again. It made me uneasy and frustrated and more than a little sad.

By Saturday morning, I'd given up on trying to catch up on homework. Instead, I decided to take a walk while the weather was nice. Going outside was risky, but I planned to stay away from the courtyard and the football field. I assumed that would keep me safe.

When I stepped out of the common room, I nearly walked right into Ty.

"Hi there." He smiled at me as he crossed his arms.

"Hi." I froze where I stood.

"Nice day, isn't it?"

"Yes." I stared at him.

"Yes, I've been waiting for you to come out."

"Seriously?" I raised an eyebrow.

"Seriously. You're not answering my texts, so I thought maybe this would be the best way to reach you. And it worked." He stepped aside. "Can we take a walk?"

"Uh, sure." I managed a quick smile. If I said no, it would make things worse. Wouldn't it?

"Great." He began to walk toward the football field.

"Where are we going exactly?" I matched his pace.

"Somewhere away from everyone else so I can prove a point." He glanced at me.

"What point is that?" I followed him onto the empty football field.

"That your problem is not with everyone, it's just with me." He caught my hand and turned me around to face him. "So, here we are. Alone. Together."

"Ty, I don't know what this is all about." I frowned.

"I think you were going to hide out all weekend just to avoid me." He stared into my eyes. "Tell me I'm wrong."

"What does it matter?"

"It matters because I want to know what the problem is. Is it because I'm on scholarship?" He narrowed his eyes.

"Are you kidding me?" I glared back at him. "Of course not. It has nothing to do with that."

"So, you admit that there is an *it*." He nodded. "Now, let's figure out what *it* is."

"I don't have to stand here and listen to this." I turned away from him and started toward the edge of the football field.

"No." He stepped in front of me to block my way. "We're going to figure this out if it takes all day."

"I said no." I glared at him. "Do you really want to argue with me again?"

"If that's what it takes." He crossed his arms. "I want to know what your problem with me is. If you're not brave enough to tell me, then I'll keep asking until you do."

"Stop it. You're being crazy." I tried to step around him again.

"No." He stepped in front of me but held up his hands. "Sorry, I'm not going to let this go any longer. It's too important to me to just keep ignoring it."

"Important to you? Why should it matter to you at all?" I took a step closer to him. "You're not going to stop me from going where I want to go."

"I will." He put his hands on my shoulders and held them there firmly as he stared into my eyes. "It's important to me, because you're important to me."

Those words stunned me. In all this time, I hadn't really considered that I might be important to him. "Why?"

"Just tell me, Apple. Just tell me what I've done to upset you." He let his hands fall away. "Then I'll let you go and you never have to see me again."

"That's just it." I took a deep breath as I looked at him. My cheeks grew hot. My stomach fluttered. "You haven't done anything to upset me. I just can't be around you. I can't think straight, I can't concentrate. It's not your fault. It's me. I've got this..." I paused, then closed my eyes. "Silly crush on you." I rushed the words out, then held my breath.

Then I felt his fingertips stroke the curve of my cheek. I

heard him whisper just beside my ear. "Breathe, Apple. I've got a silly crush too."

I opened my eyes to see his bright blue eyes staring at me intently. His cheeks were red. His voice trembled as he spoke.

"Is it really such a crazy idea? The two of us?"

NINETEEN

For a second, I wondered if I was dreaming. Was this all a fantasy I'd concocted in my head? Ty couldn't really be looking at me with that glow in his eyes—as if I'd caused it.

"Yes." I searched his eyes. "Yes, it is a crazy idea."

"Why?" His hand drifted down from my cheek and came to rest on my shoulder. "Is it because I'm not what you want me to be? Is that why you've fought so hard not to feel the way you do about me?"

"It's not you." I winced at the idea that he could think that. "Ty, you amaze me. Especially with the way that you work with kids. But it's not like we know each other well. It's not like any of this makes sense. I know what you think of me. I know that you think I'm some spoiled rich kid that couldn't possibly grasp the world you've lived in."

"You don't know anything about what I think. Nothing at all." He wrapped his hand around the back of my neck and looked straight into my eyes. "I don't care about our differences, Apple. When I look at you, I see a person that fights for what's right, that sees the invisible and doesn't let things that are wrong get swept under the rug. Yes, I want to know more about you, but that won't change the way I feel. I feel the way I do because of who you are—no matter what the rest of your story is. Do you think you could feel the same way about me?"

"I don't know your story. Not even a little." I took his free hand and gave it a gentle squeeze. "I want to, but you haven't said more than a few words about yourself to me. You tell me I hide, but I feel like you've got this wall around you, one that you won't ever let anyone cross."

"You're already on the other side." He pulled me closer as he gazed into my eyes. "I didn't invite you in—I didn't even know there was a way to get in—but one second I was alone and the next, I wasn't." He took a breath then shook his head as he exhaled. "Now that you're here, I never want to be alone again. I know you're right. It doesn't make any sense." He looked back at me. "But I don't care if it makes sense. All I know is that I want you." He whispered his words as his fingertips stroked my cheek again. "I don't want to rush it. I don't want to draw you into something that you really don't want. But I'm also not going to lie to you. I'm all in, Apple—head to toe. I'll do whatever it takes to be with you."

My heart pounded as his words echoed through my mind. Not long before, I had myself convinced that he would never want to be with me; now he spoke as if he never wanted to be without me. It was everything I wanted to hear, but at the same time, it terrified me. When he looked at me, he saw me in a way that no one ever had. When he looked at me, I was so far from invisible that there was no way for me to disappear.

The shiver that coasted up my spine—inspired by both fear and desire—took my breath away before I could speak a word. When my hand trembled with the force of it, he tightened his grasp. His lips parted just slightly as his face neared mine. Heat rushed through me as I saw his eyes drift closed and his head tilt to the side.

This was it. He was about to kiss me.

The warmth of his breath traced across my skin and I could imagine how silky his lips would be when they touched mine. My heart dropped as fear took over my desire.

"Ty." I took a step back just before his lips would have touched mine.

He looked into my eyes and in his I saw passion and confusion.

"Apple, you don't have to hide. Not from me." He tightened his grasp on my hand as his other hand brushed back through my hair, which had fallen forward to hide my face.

"Tell me something. Tell me one real thing about you." I stared back at him as my heart raced.

Yes, I wanted to kiss him. More than anything I wanted to kiss him. But the thought of kissing him before I knew who he truly was left me panicked inside.

What if I gave in to this crazy desire and the next day there was a new girl that caught his interest? He'd move on just fine and I doubted I would survive the heartbreak. And was it possible that he knew who my parents were? Had someone told him? Mick maybe? That would explain his otherwise unexplainable desire for me.

"I did. I told you how I feel about you." He pulled me close. "Isn't that enough?"

"No." I searched his eyes. "Don't you want to tell me more?"

"And prove you right? That I'm some ungrateful slacker?" He raised an eyebrow. "I'm not sure that would be a good idea."

"Are you?" My heart pounded. The closer he held me, the more I wanted to kiss him.

"Would it matter?" He smiled some.

"Maybe." I narrowed my eyes.

"I guess you'll just have to find out."

"That's what I'm trying to do, but you won't answer me." I

frowned. "You say you have feelings for me, but you're not willing to tell me the truth about yourself. How am I supposed to see that?"

"Maybe you could see it as me wanting to take time for us to get to know one another. We don't have to rush, right?"

"Maybe I could see it as you avoiding telling me anything real." I looked into his eyes. "Because you're afraid to let me see you. To let me *really* see you."

"I want you to see me." He closed his eyes, then opened them again. "There are things about me—well, I'm just not sure that you'll understand."

"Try me. Just tell me a little." I squeezed his hand. "Trust me."

"I'm all about the truth. It's important to me—that the truth is known—even if it means breaking a few rules. Even if it means getting into some trouble." He brushed the back of his hand along the curve of my cheek. "Does that satisfy your curiosity?"

"Maybe." I bit into my bottom lip. "For the moment. And I think the truth is important too."

"So, tell me the truth." His eyes locked onto mine and his arm tightened around my waist. "What are we going to do about this silly crush?"

In that moment I thought I might just lift right up off the ground. The way he looked at me left me breathless. When the moment passed, I could see the hope in his eyes.

"I think we should get to know one another and see if it might be something more."

"I think that's a great idea." He let his arm fall back to his side but he continued to hold my hand. "I've never had a silly crush before. You're my first. Please be patient with me. I might not know what to do or what to say."

"I think you're doing just fine." I smiled as I stared at him. "Let's just see where it leads."

He licked his lips, then bit into his bottom lip as he stared at me.

I could read the desire in him. He wanted to kiss me.

I wanted to kiss him too. But instead, I took a step back. I didn't want to get lost in the pounding of my heart or the ache of my lips. I wanted to know that whatever we shared was more than just a tremble in my knees and a shiver up my spine.

"I'll see you later, Ty."

"You will." He nodded as he watched me walk away.

This time he didn't try to stop me.

TWENTY

As soon as I returned to the dorm, I went straight to Maby's room. Although Candy and I had been friends for much longer, Maby had a wisdom about her that made me turn to her for advice when the situation was serious. And to me, this situation was serious. In fact, I'd never experienced anything more serious.

I knocked lightly on her door and a moment later it swung open.

"Apple, are you okay?" She pulled me inside. "You look a bit shaken."

"I'm okay." I smiled. I couldn't stop smiling. I sat down on Maby's sofa. "I'm more than okay."

"I see." She smiled too as she sat down beside me. "I'm guessing that this has something to do with Ty. Am I right?"

"Right." I took a deep breath, then blew it out from between my lips. "He told me he has a crush on me. He said he wants to see where our connection might lead. Isn't that amazing?"

"Amazing and surprising." Maby narrowed her eyes. "Did he say what he expected?"

"Not exactly. He just said that he wanted to get to know me

better, and I would like to do the same." I tilted my head to the side as I noted her strange reaction. "Why don't you look happy about this?"

"I am happy about it." She patted the back of my hand. "I'm happy if you're happy. *Are* you happy?"

"I think so." I squeezed my hands together. "I feel like the whole world is spinning around me. I feel like someone finally cares about me for real—not because of who my parents are."

"I know that's a big thing for you." Maby scooted closer to me on the sofa.

"You don't think that Mick told him, do you?" I frowned. "Maybe that's why he's interested?"

"Honey, he's interested in you because you're a gorgeous, intelligent, amazing person. That's all you need to know." She sighed.

"If that's true, then why don't you seem thrilled?"

"I'm not sure. I guess because I keep seeing love bloom right in front of me and possibly it makes me wonder about myself and my own decision to wait for romance. Plus, I do worry a little about you and Ty." She winced as she lowered her voice. "He does seem to be a bit of a troublemaker. You're the furthest thing from that."

"I know." I shook my head. "I don't know why he's always late, he's always getting detention, and now he has these service hours to do. But Candy is always getting herself detention too. She usually has a good explanation for it. He might be just trying to find his way."

"As long as you feel that you can trust him, then I support you one hundred percent." She looked into my eyes. "Do you feel that way?"

"In some ways." My heartbeat began to slow as I thought through Maby's words. "I guess I really don't know much about him. Hopefully that will change."

"I'm sure it will." Maby squeezed my hand. "Your instincts are telling you that he's the right person for you. I trust your instincts. You should too. But make sure that you find out the answers to your questions. There's nothing that troubles a relationship more than lack of trust."

"That's true." I paused as a terrible thought clouded my mind. "Do you think I'm wrong for not telling him about my family?" I met her eyes. "Do you think I'm being untrustworthy?"

"I think you're being cautious. There's nothing wrong with that. I'd love to tell you that having famous parents doesn't make a difference to people, but it does. I can't lie to you. The school has worked hard to keep your identity under wraps, and you don't want to expose yourself if you don't know for sure that Ty won't share that information with everyone."

"I don't think that he would. But you're right, I'm not sure. If I knew him just a little better, I'd feel more confident. But I don't. I just hope that he is willing to talk to me a little more. It's hard. When I'm around him, all I can think about is—"

"Okay, okay." Maby held up her hands and laughed. "I don't need the naughty details."

"Isn't it crazy?" I laughed as I blushed. "I never thought I would be in this position."

"Just keep in mind that no matter what happens between the two of you, it's natural and healthy to want to love. It's a good thing."

"I see that now. Do you?" I looked into her eyes.

"Do I? Why does that matter?" She grinned.

"You're always giving everyone advice, but you never seem interested in dating yourself. Is that because you're afraid of something?"

"Afraid?" She shrugged. "Maybe. I'm not sure it's that. I think I'd rather just wait. High school is complicated enough.

The kind of love I'm looking for—well, it's just different. I don't see myself finding it until I've graduated—maybe even from college. I'm willing to be patient."

"You're right." I rolled my eyes as I leaned back against the sofa. "High school is complicated enough and this certainly does make it even more complicated. I haven't even thought about my homework. I need to get to it. I can't lose track of everything just because Ty is running around in my head all day. If my grades drop, I won't be allowed to run the art club anymore."

"Don't stress." She patted my shoulder. "Just keep your head on straight. You'll be fine."

"Thanks, Maby." I hugged her. "I really appreciate you always being here for me. I hope I can do the same for you."

"You do." She smiled as she walked me to the door. "I love being able to help. Good luck with Ty. Just remember what I said." Her smile faded some. "Trust is very important."

"I'll remember." I stared into her eyes for a long moment, then I turned and walked away.

All the way to my dorm room, I thought about her words. Yes, trust was very important. It was amazing to think that there could be something so real and powerful between Ty and me, but without honesty to back it up, I doubted that it would last very long.

When I stepped into my dorm room, I found Candy with a bowl of popcorn in her lap.

"There you are!" She tossed some popcorn at me. "We had a movie date. Did you forget?"

"Oh, Candy, I'm so sorry." I sat down beside her. "I got caught up in something."

"In Ty?" She raised an eyebrow. "If so, I don't blame you. He's tasty."

"Stop!" I laughed and threw some popcorn back at her.

"It doesn't matter, you're here now." She snuggled up next to me and started the movie.

As I enjoyed the evening with my best friend, I realized that Ty really could be quite a distraction. If I could forget about Candy and my homework, then perhaps he was too much of a distraction.

Maby had a point. We were in high school. Could real love even happen in high school? Was it all just hormones and chemistry? What was it about Ty that I even liked?

Sure, he was good with the kids and intriguing, but what about the things I didn't like? He was always late, way too secretive, and he seemed to carry a chip on his shoulder despite the blessings he'd been given.

When I fell asleep that night, my mind was full of doubt, but my heart was full of the desire to see Ty again.

TWENTY-ONE

Instead of going right into art class, I lingered outside in the hall-way. I watched as the other students milled about, chatting as they made their way to their classes. I studied each face. But none belonged to Ty.

What was he up to that he was always so late? Was he putting in extra hours with Mick to try to improve his football skills? It crossed my mind that he might be caught up with other girls. Maybe I wasn't the only one that he'd set his sights on. Maybe he didn't want me to find out about the others.

As my mind traveled down this jealous path, I stopped myself. I had no right to be jealous. We weren't technically dating, and even if we were, we certainly weren't exclusive. But a hint of suspicion still crowded my thoughts as the second warning bell rang.

As I stepped into the classroom, Ty was officially late. It occurred to me that he might not even show up for class.

Was he avoiding me? I sat in front of my easel and pondered that possibility.

Things had gotten so intense between us so fast. I hadn't exactly been as warm as I could have been when he'd admitted that he had feelings for me. Maybe he was embarrassed. Or maybe he had realized his mistake.

As these thoughts bounced back and forth in my mind, I heard footsteps behind me. I watched as he walked past me to his easel. He didn't look at me. He kept his head down. He barely responded when Mrs. Ruby spoke to him. His shoulders slumped as he leaned forward and pretended to swipe at his canvas.

I could tell that he was pretending. Why did he even come to art class if he didn't want to create? After seeing him with the kids at art club, I knew that he had talent. But it didn't seem like art was important to him.

I couldn't even imagine living without being able to create art. It gave me an outlet, a way to express myself when words and emotions failed me.

Reminded of this, I set to work on my own painting. Again, I'd let Ty distract me. If that was going to continue, I stood to lose a lot. I could lose my future. I could lose my own artistic drive.

I could have a crush on Ty without letting it swallow me whole, couldn't I?

Determined that this would be the case, I continued to paint the building that I'd been working on for a little over a week. It was full of the people I adored the most and memories that had broken me free of my shy and closed-off nature.

Soon, I was no longer in the classroom. I'd stepped through the front door of the building, right into the room filled with pillows and curtains and lamps. In that room, I was surrounded by friends, by people I really considered family. I was safe there, even when the rest of the world left me feeling far too exposed.

"Apple." Ty paused right beside me.

"Oh!" I dropped my paintbrush and a few drops of paint

splattered up to speckle the back of his hand. "Sorry." I cringed as I grabbed a rag.

"Don't worry about it." He smiled as he wiped his hand on one of the rags stacked up on my easel.

I pulled the cloth down over my painting to hide it from his view as my heart pounded.

"I didn't realize you were there."

"Can't I see it?" He caught the edge of the cloth. "I was watching you. It was like you totally disappeared into your work. I'd love to see what it is."

"Oh, I don't really share my artwork." I cleared my throat and glanced away from him.

"But I know Mrs. Ruby considers you one of her most talented students. So, why won't you let anyone see your work?" He tugged at the edge of the cloth.

"Why were you late?" I pulled the cloth free from his grasp.

"Eh, just got delayed." He shrugged.

"Everyone else manages to make it to class on time." I bit into the tip of my tongue before I could mention the fact that most of those people appreciated the education that their parents paid small fortunes for.

"I guess I'm not everyone else." He leaned closer to me, his blond hair drifting forward until it almost tickled my cheek.

"I guess not." I whispered the words as his closeness made my heart race.

"Do you want me to be?" He met my eyes.

Everyone else in the room vanished. At least to me that's how it felt. I lost myself in those eyes that probed mine with such determination. He wanted an answer, but I could barely get myself to speak.

"No."

"You sure?" He smiled, his light blue eyes shimmering with a hint of amusement.

"I'm sure." I swallowed, then turned my attention back to the easel in front of me.

"Then show me." He stepped behind me and crouched down so that his chin nearly rested on the curve of my shoulder. "Just a quick peek."

"Ty." I sighed and started to turn to look at him, but as I did, my lips came dangerously close to his. I pulled away in the same moment that I took a sharp breath.

"Show me." He murmured his words again, this time beside my ear. "I want to see where you disappear to."

My heart raced as I realized that I wanted to show him. I wanted him to know. I wanted to invite him into my world.

"It's just a painting." I bit into my bottom lip as I pulled the cloth away. I guessed that all he would see was a random building. He wouldn't have a clue what it meant to me.

"Is that a face in the window?" He pointed to the only window where I had lightly painted a face.

"Maybe." I smiled as I looked at him. "I'm surprised you noticed."

"Not just pretty, remember?" He batted his eyes at me.

"I remember." I grinned.

"I like it. It's interesting. More than just brick and glass. It feels like another dimension." He raised an eyebrow. "But it also looks familiar. Very familiar." He looked back at me. "Is it one of the buildings here?"

My heart skipped a beat. I hadn't expected him to recognize it. Would he be able to figure out which building it was? I felt the urge to tell him not only which building it was, but what it meant to me.

As I looked into his eyes, however, I held back. How could I reveal the hideout when I wasn't sure that I could trust him?

"It's just a building." I shrugged and covered the painting up again. "Am I going to see you this afternoon?"

"Absolutely." His smile spread into a grin. "You're not going to get rid of me that easily."

"I don't want to get rid of you at all." I rose up on my toes and gave him a kiss on his cheek.

"I'm holding you to that." He wrapped his arms around me just as the bell rang. Reluctantly, he let me go as the other students began to filter out of the classroom. "See you this afternoon?"

"I'll be there." I raised an eyebrow as I met his eyes. "Will you be on time?"

"I'll do my best." He winked at me, then walked out of the classroom.

As I took my time putting my paints away, I wondered why I'd been so hesitant to tell him about the hideout. It wasn't as if my friends hadn't told others about it. It just felt as if he was hiding something from me. Maybe it was just paranoia on my part. Or maybe Ty had secrets that he would never be willing to share.

TWENTY-TWO

At the end of the day as I walked toward the bus stop, my mind was still filled with questions about Ty—and also an intense longing—a longing to be able to throw caution to the wind and kiss him the way I wanted to.

I'd seen other girls do it—friends of mine. They didn't have to think so much about things. They saw a guy they liked, and not long after they were kissing. It was simple.

But with me, it wasn't simple. What I felt for Ty wasn't simple.

I caught sight of him at the bus stop, his hands shoved into his pockets, his hoodie pulled low across his forehead. I could barely see his face, but strands of his blond hair caught the afternoon sunlight.

Did he really have to sparkle like that?

I rolled my eyes as I got closer. For once, he wasn't late. In fact, he was early.

"Hi there." I smiled at him as I walked up to him.

"Hi to you." He smiled in return.

"You're early." I glanced down the street. "The bus isn't even in sight."

"I know, I know, I'm always late." He tipped his head toward mine. "Not today, though. I'm changing my habits."

"Oh, and what brought on this change?" I looked into his eyes.

"You." He stared at me as the bus pulled up.

I pretended that I couldn't hear his answer over the roar of the engine.

"Looks like we should get going." I boarded the bus and heard him climb up the steps behind me.

What could I say to that? Was he really changing for me? Did I want him to?

As I settled in a seat, he sat down beside me.

"Is that too much?" He looked over at me.

I didn't have anywhere to hide, stuck between him and the window of the bus. I looked down at my hands clasped together in my lap. My chest ached—an indication that I'd been holding my breath.

"No." I exhaled and lifted my eyes to his. "It's surprising, though."

"I want you to know me. The real me. I'm not always late." He placed his hand on my knee and leaned closer. "There are good things about me."

"I don't doubt that." I placed my hand over his. "I'm looking forward to getting to know you."

When we arrived at the school, I felt a burst of excitement. Not just because Ty was walking right beside me—his hand wrapped around mine—but because I knew that today would be a special day for the kids in the club. I'd arranged a small art show so that they could display their latest works. It was just for other kids at the school and teachers, but it was something to give them the experience of pride in their work.

"We've got to get everything set up fast." I led Ty into the classroom. "We only have a short time to have everything on display."

"Okay, I'm on it." He began moving the easels around so that they all faced one direction. "Are you showing off one of your pieces too?"

I rolled out the paper mural that Ty and Patrick had created together. "No, this is just for the kids."

"Why is it that you won't show your art?" He grabbed one end of the paper and stretched it out across the wall.

"It's private. I just prefer to keep it that way." I taped down my end, then tossed him the roll of tape.

"Don't you think it would set a better example if you were proud of your work?" He taped down his end, then walked toward me.

"I didn't say I wasn't proud. I just said it was private." I shrugged and turned toward the stack of fliers I'd prepared to hand out that day.

"Saying it's private isn't really saying anything at all, is it?" He paused just behind me.

I knew that if I turned around, I'd end up looking into his eyes. I'd be trapped by the intensity of them, the way they could dive right into me and seek out places I wasn't ready to reveal. I remained where I stood.

"It's saying that what I create is for me, not for anyone else."

"But why? Aren't we supposed to be getting to know each other?" He smiled some.

"I seem to be the only one answering the questions." I crossed my arms as I looked at him.

"Okay, a question for a question." He smiled at me. "You first. Why don't you want to show your art?"

"And I'm supposed to believe that you're going to answer one of my questions after I answer one of yours?" I shook my head. "I'm not that stupid."

"Ouch, that's harsh, Apple." He narrowed his eyes and shifted closer to me. "You can't trust me even a little?"

"Fine." My heart pounded as I settled my hand on his chest. "I'm trusting you. Just a little bit. I don't like to share my art because it belongs to me. It's pretty much the only thing that is just mine. My parents—well, they don't exactly support the idea of me being an artist. When I was younger and shared my art with them, their responses were not encouraging."

"I'm so sorry." He frowned. "That must have been heart-breaking to hear."

"It wasn't." I shrugged. "That's just them. They are very practical people. They want me to live a certain lifestyle. So, art is not my future, but that doesn't mean I don't love it. There's no reason to enter art shows or to display my art and open it up for criticism when it's just a hobby that's meant for me to enjoy."

"When art runs through your blood, it's not something that you can hide." He glanced toward the door as a few kids began to enter. "Looks like we're out of time."

"That's not fair." I frowned as I met his eyes. "I still get my question."

"Of course." He grinned, then turned to greet the kids.

As I watched him interact with the kids, I was reminded once more of how tender he was with them. He put on such a tough shell around everyone else, but with the kids, he was nothing but silly and kind.

Once the artwork was arranged and the teachers and other students began to parade through the classroom to have a look, I watched the kids that stood beside their work. They each beamed with pride. I couldn't ignore a subtle longing within me to feel the same way.

Ty had been right. I did want to show my art. I did want others to see it. But I didn't think I could handle the rejection that would come with it. What if someone discovered who my parents were and only pretended to like my art for that reason? There simply was no way for me to know for sure.

I watched Ty showing off the mural that he and Patrick had created. I saw pride in him too, but not for his own work—for Patrick's. It made me wonder if he'd been like Patrick when he was younger. Maybe that would be the question that I asked him.

I wanted to know where he disappeared to—what always made him late—but I also wanted to know what had turned him into the person he was. I felt as if it might be the only question he'd ever willingly answer.

After saying goodbye to the students and cleaning up the easels, I caught Ty walking toward the door.

"Oh no!" I grabbed him by the arm and pulled him back toward me. "You owe me an answer."

"Not here." He grinned as he pulled his arm free. "After we get back to Oak Brook, okay?"

"Okay." I frowned. I didn't want to wait any longer, but I did have to get the classroom cleaned up and then the bus would be busy on the way back to Oak Brook. I did my best to be patient, but by the time we stepped off the bus, my patience had run thin.

"Okay, we're alone now." I took his hand as we stepped off the bus.

"Not exactly." He winced as he looked over at Mitch and a few other football players who waited at the entrance of Oak Brook Academy. "Did I forget to mention we have an extra practice today?"

"Unbelievable." I crossed my arms as I looked at him.

"I'm not avoiding it, I swear." He looked into my eyes. "After practice. Okay?"

"After practice." I sighed as I watched him join the others.

For someone who wasn't avoiding my questions, he did run away pretty quickly.

TWENTY-THREE

To pass the time without losing my mind, I decided I'd pour my emotions into a painting. I grabbed a small canvas from my room and a portable easel. I didn't often paint outside—mainly because I didn't like anyone to get a glimpse of what I created—but the balmy air called to me.

I set my easel up on a picnic table in the courtyard and began to paint. It didn't surprise me when an image of Ty entered my mind. Yes, I wanted to paint him. But I needed a distraction, not an obsession.

I took a deep breath, cleared my mind, and began to paint again. What emerged from the tip of my paintbrush was something unexpected.

Usually I created art that represented real things—buildings, landscapes, people. But this time, what spilled across the canvas was a vibrant star. It shimmered brilliantly against a dark blue background.

As I watched it come alive with strokes of gold paint across the canvas, I wondered where it had come from. What part of me wanted to paint this star?

There was a time when I'd spend hours stargazing, but I'd

forgotten about that habit. It was before I'd come to Oak Brook Academy, before I had to do my best to hide who I was.

I thought about the telescope my father had bought for me when I was only eight. He'd mounted it on one of the balconies of our house and it had given a clear view of the stars. I used to spend hours imagining what it would be like to travel through space and maybe even discover some new worlds.

As I set my paintbrush down, I smiled at the image and the nostalgia it stirred in me. No, it wasn't my best work and it wouldn't mean much to anyone but me, but I was glad that I'd painted it.

"Wow, that's really beautiful." Ty's voice drifted over one of my shoulder.

"Ty!" I frowned as I covered up the canvas.

"Stop." He drew the cloth back and stared at the star. "Why would you ever want to hide something like that?"

"It's my turn for questions, remember?" As I turned to face him, I realized that the last of the afternoon light had begun to fade.

"I remember." He cleared his throat as he looked at me. "I'm here, aren't I?"

"Yes." I took his hand. "And I'm so glad that you are."

"I'm happy to hear you say that." He stared into my eyes. "I wasn't sure if you'd be waiting for me."

"You thought I'd have something better to do?" I laughed.

"I thought maybe you'd come to your senses." He brushed my hair back from my eyes.

"I might think the same thing about you." I tightened my grasp on his hand. "I'm ready to ask my question, Ty."

"Go for it." He exhaled as his hand fell back to his side.

"Why won't you tell me where you go? Why you're always late?" I looked into his eyes. "What are you hiding from me?"

"That's three questions." He winced and drew his hand

away from mine. "This doesn't have to be so serious. Isn't there something else you'd like to ask?" He took a few steps back from me.

"Ty." I sighed as I watched him. "You promised me you'd answer."

"I did." He licked his lips. "But aren't I entitled to some privacy? Why do you need to know? It's my business, right?"

"Now you're getting angry at me?" I took a step back of my own and narrowed my eyes. "You're the one that made the promise. Why can't you just answer me?"

"I will. Anything else?" He shook his head. "Do you want to know my most embarrassing moment? How about my first kiss? I mean, those are all options."

"I asked you the question I wanted to ask already." I placed my hands on my hips. "If you weren't going to answer, you should have just told me. I'm not interested in playing games."

"It's not a game!" He snapped his words as he turned away from me. "That's the problem. You think everything is so simple, because it's been simple for you. It's not simple for everyone."

"Fine. Don't answer then. Tell me I can't possibly understand because I'm just too spoiled, right?" I crossed my arms and glared at his back. "Then why bother with someone like me—if I'm too stupid and naive to be honest with?"

"I'm afraid. Is that what you want to hear?" He turned to face me, his face a mask of emotion as he locked his eyes to mine. "You scare me."

"Me?" I stared back at him. "How could I possibly scare you?"

"How?" He chuckled as he shook his head. "You can't figure that out?"

"I shouldn't have to. You should just be able to tell me." I crossed some of the distance between us but left some space as a buffer. I didn't want to lose myself in his touch, to be distracted by his breath on my skin or his whisper in my ear. "Trust me, Ty. I'm here. I'm not going anywhere."

"You're here right now." He took a step toward me. "You're here because of the things I don't tell you. But the moment that changes, you're going to be gone. I'll be just a memory to you, but you'll be much more than that to me."

"How can you just assume that you know how I feel?"

"I can assume that I know how your mind works." He touched my temple, his fingertips hot against my tender skin. "That's all I need to know."

"You don't."

"I do." He searched my eyes. "It's never been challenged, not by anything real. Everything is still so black and white for you."

"If I'm so sheltered, if I'm so black and white, then why even waste your time with me?" I pushed his hand away and frowned. "Maybe if you didn't spend so much time looking down on me, you'd actually get to know me."

"I'm not looking down." He narrowed his eyes. "I'm just being honest."

"So, this you can be honest about? Insulting me? That warrants the truth. But answering a simple question, that's a problem?" I shook my head. "Ty, I think you're fascinating, but all you seem to think of me is that I'm limited and naive."

"That's not true." He caught my hand and closed his fingers around it. "I think you're amazing."

"You certainly don't act like it." I took a breath. "If I'm so wonderful then why can't you trust me with your secrets? Why can't you trust that maybe I could understand?"

"I just can't risk it." He whispered as he crossed the final distance between us. "Can't you understand that, Apple? What we have..." He trailed his hand through the strands of my hair that tumbled into my face. "It's too precious."

"Without trust, what do we have?" I held my breath as I felt the warmth of his hand tangled in my hair. I wanted the sensation to continue. I wanted him to pull me into his arms and never let me go, but I knew that could never happen. Not while he held back from me. Not while I sensed that this might not be more than just a little fun for him.

"Each other, this moment, this…" His palm slid out of my hair and down along the curve of my cheek. As he tipped my chin up with the heel of his palm, his lips neared mine.

My heartbeat quickened, then leaped and stole my breath before I could fully take it. I felt the brush of his lips—just a light tickle, with a promise of more. My lips trembled as I pulled back from the caress.

"No." I took another step back as he opened his eyes to look at me.

I could see the disappointment. The frustration and the desire mixed together to create a shadow in those eyes' light blue color.

"No?" He reached for me again and pulled me close, though he didn't try to kiss me. "Why? You don't want to kiss me?"

"I do." I shivered with the force of how much I wanted to kiss him. "But not like this."

"Like what?" He glanced around the courtyard. "Here, alone in the dark?"

"Here—alone, but not trusting each other." I frowned and braced myself for his reaction. Would he think I was ridiculous for wanting things a certain way? "Ty, I don't want to just kiss you. I could just kiss any guy. I want more than that with you. I want our first kiss to be honest."

"Honest." He whispered the word as he smiled. "You really are fascinating, you know that?" He brushed my hair back from my face and stroked my cheeks in the process. "Apple, I never expected to find you, but now that I have, I'll do anything to not lose you."

"Anything but tell me the truth?" I stared into his eyes.

"Give me time." His smile faded as he exhaled. "Can you do that? Can you give me just a little time?"

"I can." I nodded and wrapped my arms around him. As I hugged him, I imagined wrapping the love I felt for him all around him. I wanted to protect him from everything that scared him, from whatever it was that he thought he couldn't tell me.

I wished there was a way that I could wipe away the fear that held him back from me. But for the moment, it would just have to be a hug.

TWENTY-FOUR

After another restless night, I felt exhausted as I trudged down the hall to my first class. The thought of seeing Ty again gave me enough energy to push open the door, but that excitement soon faded when I noticed that he wasn't in the classroom. It shouldn't have surprised me, since he was often late, but I did feel a little disappointed.

That worried me. How had I gotten so wrapped up in him? It was strange to think that just his absence was enough to leave me feeling empty and uncertain. How could I feel so strongly about him when I had no idea if he felt the same way about me? All my life I'd had to be so careful about who I let get too close. Now I wanted him beside me more than anything, but I had no idea if I could trust him.

As the class neared its end, Ty finally made an appearance. His hair was ruffled and his hands looked red and raw, as if he'd scrubbed them. I couldn't take my eyes off them as he sat down beside me.

"Late?" I looked up at him.

"Crazy morning." He rubbed his hands together.

I caught the scent of soap as it drifted through the air above his hands.

"Seems like it." I tipped my head toward him. "Are you going to tell me about it?"

"Maybe after class." He slid his hands into his pockets.

"Maybe." I sighed as I looked back at Mrs. Ruby, who stood at the front of the room. I did my best to lose myself in her instructions.

As the class neared an end, the topic shifted to the upcoming art show. Mrs. Ruby had been pleading with me for over a month to enter a piece of my work, but I'd refused. The more pressure she placed on me, the more I resisted. It frustrated me that she wouldn't just take no for an answer. I felt some relief when she didn't mention me as she described the work that would be on display. As soon as class was over, however, she cornered me. While all the other students left—including Ty—she did her best to keep my attention.

"I just need a little help putting things away today. Don't worry, I'll give you a note to take to your next class."

"Sure." I frowned as I realized that Ty had managed to evade me again. As soon as Mrs. Ruby and I were alone, she directed me to some canvases she needed put away and focused in on the art show.

"Listen, I want this art show to go very well. If it does, then we might be able to get a little more funding for the arts program that you run. We might be able to expand it to other schools."

"I think that's fantastic." I smiled as I stacked up the canvases. "I'm sure it will go well."

"Maybe. But I know it would go a lot better if I could put a piece of your work on display." She looked into my eyes. "Just one piece Apple. It would be such a wonderful addition to what we already have. I'm sure that Mr. Fein, who runs the enhanced art program, would accept you into the program in a second as soon as he sees your work."

"I don't want to be in that program, Mrs. Ruby." I sighed as I looked at her. "I know that you're trying to be nice and it does mean a lot to me, but this isn't something that I want to do. I hope that you can understand that."

"I suppose I have no choice." She frowned. "I just want to be sure that you know how talented you are. That's what's important to me, Apple."

"Thanks." I smiled at her, then carried the canvasses to the storage closet.

Her words did mean a lot to me, but her praise also left me feeling uneasy. Yes, there was a part of me that wanted to follow my dream of becoming an artist, but that was something I had to find a way to ignore, as it wasn't a possibility. The more Mrs. Ruby brought it up, the harder it was to ignore it.

I stepped into the closet and carried the canvasses over to a shelf against the back wall. As I set them on the shelf, I heard the sound of the door closing behind me.

"Don't worry, I've got this." I turned around to face Mrs. Ruby.

Instead, I found Ty right inside the door.

"She went to speak with the principal." He walked toward me. "I heard the two of you talking."

"You mean you were listening in?" I met his eyes as I leaned back against the shelf behind me.

"Maybe." He shrugged. "I thought you would have a better explanation for her than you did for me—about why you don't want your artwork out there." He raised an eyebrow. "Have you ever considered that you're being selfish?"

"Selfish?" I stared at him. "You came in here to insult me?"

"No." He leaned his shoulder against the shelf beside me and looked into my eyes. "I came in here to speak some truth."

"Your truth." I crossed my arms. "Your version."

"Not my version. The truth." He shifted a little closer to me. "What you create—it's not meant just for your eyes. I think you know that."

"I don't know that." I tightened my arms across my chest and took a slow breath.

"You do." He lowered his voice as he searched my eyes. "You can feel it, can't you? When you're creating something, it's more than just paint on canvas, isn't it?"

"I don't know what you mean." I closed my eyes.

"We're alone here." He placed a hand gently on the curve of my elbow. His arm stretched across my crossed arms.

I could feel the warmth of his forearm through the thin material of my shirt. He tugged my elbow just enough to guide me to turn toward him.

As I did, my eyes fluttered open and I found him staring at me. "Ty. I have so much to do."

"No, you don't." He released my elbow and tucked my hair behind my ear instead. "You have this moment—just you and me. That's all we have to do."

"I wish that was the case." I shook my head.

"Apple, you decide where you want to be and how you want to spend your time. I'm not asking for it for me, though I'd like to." He smiled. "I'm asking for it for you. Because it's time you figured out what's holding you back. You can tell me that you don't feel it, but I know that you're lying to me. I know what it's like to create something. I know how it feels when it pushes out from the inside and screams to exist. It isn't born just to please you, it's born for everyone." He stared straight into my eyes. "Are you going to tell me that you don't feel that?"

I held my breath. I had no choice. If I'd taken a breath, I might have exhaled everything that I'd been keeping pent up inside. I might have spilled out the truth about the sleepless nights, about the yearning I had to share my art, about the sadness that washed over me whenever I looked into my closet full of canvasses and creations. How could I admit to something that I'd been working so hard to ignore?

"Apple." He ran his hand along my cheek, then touched the back of my neck.

For an instant, I thought he might kiss me. The way he guided my face closer to his ignited a storm of desire within me.

"Breathe." He smiled as his lips came to rest on my forehead.

The warmth of his kiss sent a shiver through my body.

I closed my eyes, startled by the intensity of my reaction to his affection, and I had no choice but to draw a sharp breath.

TWENTY-FIVE

"That's better." He rested his forehead against mine and closed his eyes. "Not everything has to be so scary, you know." His hands ran down the length of my arms, then curled around mine with a gentle squeeze. "I just want you to know you're not alone in all this."

"I'm not?" I tried to study his face as his eyes remained closed. His intoxicating scent, the nearness of his lips—it all left my heart pounding and my knees weak. But I wanted more than just the dizziness that left me unable to form a complete thought. I wanted him to open his eyes and his heart to me.

"No." He drew his head back, then opened his eyes. "You may not believe me, but you're not alone."

"I want to believe you." I tipped my head back as I searched his eyes. "So why were you late for class?"

"Apple." He sighed, then ran his hand back through his hair. His hoodie slipped back and settled against his shoulders and back.

I noticed streaks of red paint that stood out against his golden hair.

"Were you painting?" I smiled at the thought.

"Huh?" He tugged his hoodie back up over his head.

"There's paint in your hair." I laughed as I coiled a strand of his hair around my finger and tugged it. "Don't act like it isn't there."

"Yeah, I was painting." He looked into my eyes, then glanced away. "Sometimes I get into a flow and I lose track of time."

"Where's your painting? I want to see it." I wrapped my hand around his. "Please?"

"It's not ready yet." He offered a tight smile. "I promise, I'll show you when it's ready."

"Can I believe that?" I looked straight into his eyes before he could turn away.

"Yes. You can." He brought the back of my hand to his lips and kissed it. "But right now, I have to go."

"Okay." I frowned as he pulled away.

I was tempted to make up anything to convince him to stay. But I decided against it. He clearly still needed his space. He'd given me a little, but I hoped that soon he would feel comfortable enough to give me a lot more.

Ty painted in secret?

My heart skipped a beat. Maybe we had more in common than I realized.

For the remainder of the day I thought about what he might have created. Something with plenty of red paint. Maybe a stop sign? A firetruck? Maybe even a heart? The thought made me smile.

"You're really losing it now, Apple." I rolled my eyes as I walked toward the bus stop after school. But my imagination still filled with images of Ty painting a giant heart with our names in the middle.

Sure, it was a little silly, but I couldn't help it. I'd never felt this way about anyone before. He seemed to feel the same way, but he hadn't exactly made that clear.

He still wanted to keep secrets. And the truth was, so did I.

As I waited at the bus stop, I wondered if his painting would be ready. Would he bring it with him? Take me to it? I tried to envision where he painted. The dorms were big and the bedrooms were large enough to paint in, but I doubted that he would paint there, especially if he wanted privacy.

I glanced at my watch again. Seconds had turned into minutes. If he didn't show up soon, the bus would come and go without him. Maybe he was painting, but that was no excuse—not when it came to the kids.

Just when I thought he was taking his responsibilities more seriously, this happened. Maybe I was just expecting too much. He'd been late plenty of times before. This time, though, I couldn't help but wonder if it was because of the moment we'd shared.

Were things happening too fast for him? Had he decided to back off and maybe not help with the kids at all anymore? Maybe pressuring him to show me his art had pushed him away. It would push me away from most people.

I chewed on my bottom lip as I thought about the night before. He'd admitted to me that he was afraid, and instead of comforting him, I'd demanded to know why. Maybe if I'd been more under-standing, he would have showed up on time for the bus.

I craned my neck as I looked toward the school. If I caught a glimpse of him, I could ask the driver to wait. Instead, I saw a few leaves blow across the sidewalk.

Frustrated, I looked back down the street. I heard the rumble of the bus before I spotted it. Another glance over my shoulder revealed no sign of Ty. With my stomach in knots I walked toward the edge of the sidewalk. What did this mean?

Was he done with me? The kids? How could I know when he was never exactly clear with me?

As the bus came to a stop, I stepped up into it at the same moment that sirens shrieked through the air. Startled, I looked back out at the sidewalk.

Ty ran right past the bus, his hoodie blown back by the force of his speed. A police car squealed to a stop right in front of the bus and two police officers jumped out onto the sidewalk.

As I watched, they chased Ty down the sidewalk. Shocked, I considered just for a moment the possibility of running after them. But that moment passed when the doors of the bus slammed shut.

"Don't know what that's all about, but you don't want to get in the middle of it, young lady." The driver tipped his head at me.

My heart slammed against my chest. What was it all about? What had Ty done that caused the police to chase after him?

As I watched, one of the officers managed to catch up to Ty. In one leap, the officer knocked him to the ground. The other officer stepped up to handcuff Ty, who thrashed and struggled against the process.

My stomach churned with fear. Would they hurt him? Would they shoot him? He certainly wasn't cooperating.

The first officer tugged him to his feet and led him back toward the police car. As they walked past the bus, Ty glanced up just in time to meet my eyes through the doors. I held my breath as he looked away. How could this be happening? A part of me wanted to force my way through the door, to demand that he be released, but I had no real authority to do that. Instead, I only watched as the officer shoved him into the back of the police car.

As the car pulled away, I felt my muscles grow weak.

"Ty." I whispered his name as the bus lurched forward.

"Take your seat, we've got to make up for some time." The bus driver shot me a stern look.

I sank down into the nearest seat and held back a sob. Could Ty really be a criminal? Had I overlooked the signs because I'd gotten so lost in who I hoped he was?

TWENTY-SIX

By the time I hung up the phone, the bus had reached my stop. As I stepped off of it, my head spun. No one I'd spoken to knew why Ty had been arrested, not even Mick.

The memory of him being led to the police car haunted me. I felt as if I should have done something to help him. But what could I have done? I couldn't stop the police from arresting him. I couldn't stop him from doing whatever it was he'd done that made the police chase him.

Still, as I did my best to stay calm through the art club, I couldn't stop thinking about him.

"Apple." Patrick tugged at the edge of my shirt. "Where's Ty?"

I sighed as I looked into his eyes. I could tell him the truth— that I'd allowed a criminal to be part of our group. I'd exposed all these children to his influence, even though my instincts had warned me against it from the beginning. Maybe I should have listened.

"He can't be here today. But I know how much he enjoyed working with you on your project. Do you need some help with it?" I smiled at him.

"No. It's okay." He frowned, then walked back over to his easel.

My heart ached for him. I understood that sense of disappointment and confusion. Ty had a way of reaching into people and his absence left a definite hole.

After all the kids had left and everything was cleaned up, I pulled out my phone again. I'd tried to forget about the fact that he was in jail. I'd tried to convince myself that it wasn't my place to do anything about it. But the truth was, I knew I couldn't last another minute with him behind bars.

I sat down on the edge of the desk in the front of the classroom with my phone. As I dialed a familiar number, I wondered what kind of response I'd get. I knew he would do what I asked, but I guessed that he would give me a hard time about it.

"Apple, I haven't heard from you lately. I thought you must be busy. How are you? How is school?"

"It's fine." I cleared my throat.

"What's up? Something's wrong. What is it?" His voice grew stern.

"Dad, I need your help with something." I braced myself.

"What is it? Anything, you know that. Anything at all."

"A friend of mine got himself into some trouble."

"Mick? What did he do now?"

"No, not Mick." I took a breath. "He's a new friend."

"A new friend? Not sure I like the sound of this. Did you have Davis run a background check on him?"

"Dad, please. I just need your help. He's been arrested and I want to make sure that he's released. Can you do that for me?" I held my breath. My parents were both overprotective of me and I doubted that hearing my new friend was currently in jail would make him very happy.

"Apple, I don't know what you've gotten yourself in the

middle of, but this is not acceptable. Where did you meet this boy?"

"At school, Dad. He goes to Oak Brook too. He's not a bad person. He just needs a little help. Can you please help him?"

"Oh, Apple." He sighed. "You know I'll do anything for you, but this is a bit much. If he's in jail, it's because he committed a crime."

"You know that's not always true, Dad. I don't know what he did, but it couldn't have been that bad. He's a good person." I swallowed hard as I hoped that was the case. I didn't often ask my parents to wield their influence, but in this case, I couldn't not ask.

"If you say he is, I believe you. But this is not the kind of person I want you spending time with. If I help this boy out, I expect that you'll steer clear of him. Understand?"

I rolled my eyes and held back a sigh. "Sure, whatever you say, Dad. Will you help him?"

"No, not whatever I say. I mean it, Apple. You may think he's a great guy, but he did something to get himself arrested, didn't he? That's not the kind of person you should be around. You know how everything we do is scrutinized, that's why we fought so hard to find you a school where you could have as much freedom to be yourself as possible. But there are still rules that you have to follow and one of those rules is not getting involved with people that could bring you unwanted attention."

"Yes, Dad." I closed my eyes. I knew the rules very well. I'd been living with them all my life. At the moment, it didn't matter. All I wanted was for Ty to be free and safe. I'd deal with the consequences later. "Will you help, please?"

"Of course I will. Give me the information."

I relayed Ty's name and the police department that had taken him into custody. "Thanks, Dad."

"Just remember the rules, Apple. It's important. I know at your age you can't grasp the full—"

"I'll remember, Dad." I bit into my bottom lip.

As grateful as I was that he was willing to help, I felt more alone than ever. How could he ever understand the way that I felt about Ty? His world was so different from mine. While my parents attended glamorous parties and had their names and faces splashed across magazines and newspapers, I had to hide. Always hide.

If the press found out I attended Oak Brook Academy, they would surround the school until they got a glimpse of me.

Even if it meant that I'd never get to speak to Ty again, I was glad that I'd called my father. He had the connections to get Ty released. And maybe he was right. Maybe I just couldn't grasp the risk of knowing Ty. I'd given him every opportunity to share his secrets with me, but instead, he'd gotten himself into serious trouble. Obviously, he didn't take what had developed between us seriously. In fact, I doubted that he was giving me a second thought.

My heart ached on the bus ride back to Oak Brook Academy. I'd believed in him. That was the hardest part. I'd believed in him and I'd believed him when he said that he cared. But it was all just part of whatever game he was playing.

As I walked through the door of my dorm room, my phone began to ring. I saw his name on the caller ID. That meant that he was out. I sat down on the sofa and sent the call to voicemail. A few seconds later, a text appeared.

APPLE, we need to talk.

"I'LL BET." I rolled my eyes, then tucked my phone into my

pocket. My father and I didn't agree on a lot of things, but this time, I wondered if he might be right.

The door swung open and Candy walked in.

"There you are!" She sat down beside me. "I tried to get back before you got here. I can't believe what happened." She threw her arms around me. "Are you okay?"

"I'm fine." I hugged her back. "I guess the whole school knows."

"Not as far as I can tell. We've been doing our best to keep it under wraps." Candy stared into my eyes. "I'm not worried about that. What I want to know is how you're doing. It must have been such a shock to see that happen."

"It was." I clenched my hands into fists. "I didn't know what to do. Maybe I should have gotten off of the bus."

"What could you have done?" She shook her head. "Nothing. You did the right thing."

"You think that, but will he?" I shook my head as I stared down at my hands. "Why do I even care what he thinks? Obviously, he isn't the person that I thought he was to begin with."

"You don't know what really happened." Candy shrugged. "Maybe it was a misunderstanding."

"If it was a misunderstanding, why would he be running from the police? Why wouldn't he just explain what happened?" I stood up from the sofa and crossed my arms. "No, I think I'm the one who made a mistake here. I wanted to see something in him that just isn't there. I should have trusted my first instincts." I took a deep breath, then walked toward the door. "I think I just need to do my best to forget him."

TWENTY-SEVEN

There was only one place for me to go, one place where I could truly feel a sense of peace if I tried hard enough. With my father's words echoing through my mind, I headed for the hideout. I hoped Mick and Alana wouldn't be wrapped up in each other's arms when I walked in. I couldn't stand the sight of seeing them together when my own heart felt like it had been smashed into thousands of pieces.

When I pushed through the door, I was relieved to find that the hideout was empty. I stepped up to the face I'd painted over not long before. I knew it was Ty. No one else did.

As I stared at the outline covered up by streaks of paint, my heart ached. My hand shook as I picked up a paintbrush and began to paint the same image again. Was the light I'd seen in his eyes real? Had I just imagined it?

I took a deep breath and looked out the window in an attempt to calm my nerves. But breathing deep made me think of Ty's reminders to breathe. He could always tell when I was holding my breath. No one had ever done that for me before. When I was with him, I felt as if I could unfurl, that I could stretch out all of me and not worry about the consequences.

But that was the Ty I'd imagined. The real Ty, the one that had been led away in handcuffs—that was the one that didn't care who he hurt. I looked back at the image on the wall and stared into the bright blue eyes that I'd created. I felt a subtle shiver race up my spine, as it was almost as if I could feel him staring back at me. Goosebumps popped up along my skin as I continued to feel watched.

Nervous, I turned around and discovered the same blue eyes staring at me.

"Ty!" I dropped my paintbrush on the floor and did my best to hide the painting on the wall.

"Apple, please, just give me a chance to explain." He walked toward me.

"No! You shouldn't be here!" I glared at him. "Did you follow me?"

"You wouldn't answer my texts or my calls. I was hanging out outside the dorms, hoping I might catch you. I saw you run through the courtyard and yes, I followed you." He shoved his hands in his pockets and frowned. "This place is exactly how you drew it. Even your face in the window was the same."

"You've been here that long?" My stomach twisted as I realized there was no point in hiding what I'd painted. He'd seen me creating it.

"Yes." He took a step closer, so that we were only inches apart. "Apple, what you saw today—"

"No." I cut him off before he could continue. "I don't want to hear it. I've had enough of you telling me stories. I can't trust anything you say to me. I want you to go!"

"Don't." He cupped my cheek as he shook his head. "Don't push me away. I know that's not what you want."

"It is." I pulled away from his touch and backed right into the painting on the wall.

"Then why did you invite me here?" He murmured the

question as he placed his hand on the wall over my shoulder and looked into my eyes. "Why did you paint me on your wall?"

"You're not the one that gets to ask questions!" I glared at him. "Why did you get arrested? Why were you running from the police?"

"I can't exactly tell you." He frowned.

"No." I stared into his eyes. "No, you're not getting away with that this time. Either you tell me right now or this—whatever it is—is over."

"Don't say that." He narrowed his eyes as he looked at me. "Apple, you don't have to trust me, but if you want me to tell you the truth, then you have to let me show you something."

"Why can't you just tell me?"

"It's impossible to explain—not the way you want me to. If you want to know everything, you've got to let me show you. Will you come with me?" He held his hand out to me, his fingers outstretched. "Please?"

My heart pounded as my mind resisted the urge to grab his hand. No, I shouldn't go anywhere with him. No, I shouldn't long to be in his arms.

"Yes." I took his hand as I looked into his eyes. "I want to know the truth, Ty."

"I'll show you." He squeezed my hand, then led me out of the building.

As we slipped out through the entrance of Oak Brook Academy, I felt a hint of fear. It didn't make any sense to go with him. He'd just been released from jail. I still had no idea why he'd been arrested. What if he intended to hurt me?

As if he could sense my worry, Ty met my eyes. He didn't speak, he just stared into them. He didn't have to say a word.

Maybe I didn't know everything there was to know about Ty, but I did know that he wouldn't do anything to hurt me.

He led me through alleys until he reached a street not far from the bus stop. He turned to face me.

"I've never shown anyone this before."

"What?" I looked around the alley. Other than a few dumpsters, it was empty.

"Apple, I know that what happened today had to be scary for you and I'm sorry that you had to see it, but this is part of who I am." He took my hand and guided me around the corner of the alley. There, on the sprawling surface of a large building, a mural stood out in the last of the evening light.

I held my breath as I drank in the images. They were familiar. It took me only a second to realize that they were the various art pieces that the students at the art club had created.

"You did this?" I whispered my words as I took in the details of the mural.

"I've been working on it. I create my art whenever I can—that's why I'm always running late. I have to work when no one can catch me." He pushed his hoodie back and looked at the mural. "I got caught in the middle of this one. I just wanted to cover up some of this graffiti with something positive. I thought maybe if the kids from the art program saw it, they'd know that someone believed in them."

"Ty." I turned to look at him in the same moment that he tugged me closer. As our bodies neared each other, I felt a surge of desire for him—for this artist that I thought I knew who had an entirely secret world.

"Apple, I don't want to hide things from you." He rested his forehead against mine. "I want to share everything with you."

They were the words I wanted to hear, but as his arms wrapped around me—as I felt the warmth of his touch and sensed the closeness of his lips—I drew back. I pulled away until he released his grasp on me.

"But you didn't." I looked into his eyes as he stared back at me. "You didn't tell me about any of this. Not until you got caught. Not until you had to. How am I supposed to believe that this is the only secret you have?" I shook my head, despite the ache in my heart. "You ran from the police. You put yourself at risk and I'm just supposed to accept that? I'm sorry, Ty, but I can't. You had so many chances to tell me the truth."

"So did you." He raised an eyebrow as he studied me.

"I didn't lie to you."

"No?" He brushed his hand back through my hair, pushing it away from my face. "I know who got me out of jail, Apple. I know what you've been hiding from me. I was not the only one hiding things, was I?"

I pushed his hand away as I frowned. "I had my reasons."

"So did I." He crossed his arms.

"Ty, we can't do this." I took a sharp breath as the force of my words struck me before I even spoke them. "We can't trust each other. If we don't trust each other we don't have anything."

"Apple, don't." He reached for my hand.

I pulled it away and ran off down the alley. I had to get back to Oak Brook. I had to get back to the only place where I ever felt safe.

TWENTY-EIGHT

No matter how hard I tried, I couldn't sleep. Sunlight peeked through my window after hours of tossing and turning. All I could think of was Ty and just how much I disliked him. He'd coaxed me into falling in love with him. It was one hundred percent his fault. Until he'd gotten involved in my life, I'd been just fine.

I punched my pillow and shoved my head underneath it. I didn't want to get out of bed. I didn't want to see anyone, especially not him. When my phone buzzed, I ignored it. I guessed that it would be more texts from him. I'd been ignoring them all night. Each word he sent only made my frustration grow.

However, it wasn't really him I was angry at. I was the one that had let myself get lost in a fantasy.

When my phone began to ring, I finally picked it up. Instead of Ty, it was Mrs. Ruby.

My stomach twisted. The art show. I'd promised her that I would at least show up for it.

I was reminded of Ty's insisting that we attend together. I doubted that he would dare to show his face there now.

"Hi, Mrs. Ruby." I sighed as I pressed the phone against my ear.

"Hi, Apple. I just wanted to say thank you so much. I'm really excited for you. I can't wait to see you at the art show."

"You're welcome." I rubbed my eyes as I sat up in my bed. I hadn't done much to help, but I knew that Mrs. Ruby appreciated any help that she could get. "I'll be there soon."

My choices were to hide out in my dorm room or to go to the one place I knew he wouldn't be.

After his run-in with the cops, I was sure Mrs. Ruby wouldn't want him to be involved in the arts program anymore. If she didn't know about it yet, I'd make sure that she found out.

How could I have trusted him to set a good example for the kids in the program while he was out committing crimes the entire time? I'd never seen graffiti as art, though I knew that some people viewed it that way.

The memory of Ty's creation, however, did haunt me as I got dressed for the day. His recreation of their artwork combined with the message he wanted to send them still struck me as a very beautiful thing. But he didn't have to choose to express himself in an illegal way. He didn't have to be part of the problem instead of part of the solution, even after everything he'd been given. He had an opportunity that the kids in the arts program could only dream about, and instead of being grateful, he had put it all at risk. That was not something I could ever understand.

When I arrived at the art show, I did my best to put on a brave face. I didn't want the world to know that Ty had broken my heart. Most of all, I didn't want Mrs. Ruby to know. I admired her as a teacher, but a part of me felt annoyed that she'd thrust Ty into my world in the first place. No, it wasn't her fault, but she had been part of it, hadn't she?

"Oh, Apple! I'm so glad that you're finally here!" Mrs. Ruby rushed toward me with a wide smile. "I've been dying for you to arrive so that I could introduce you to a few people."

"People? Why?" I met her eyes as my heart began to race. I generally preferred to blend into the background instead of meeting new people.

"They just love your work, Apple. Trust me, you're going to be happy to meet them." She grabbed my hand and started to pull me through the crowd of people.

"My work? What are you talking about?"

"Here she is!" Mrs. Ruby called out. "The artist is finally here!"

The artist? My heart jumped into my throat. She couldn't be talking about me, could she?

My head swam as I attempted to put together what might have happened. Before I could even begin to, my eyes locked onto a painting on the wall in front of me. Several people had gathered near it to observe the building and each detail in the several windows that lined it from the first floor to the roof.

My stomach twisted and I felt the blood drain from my face.

"How?" I stammered out the word.

Mrs. Ruby spoke to me and to the others nearby, but I didn't hear her words. I couldn't hear anything but the pounding of my heart in my ears.

"Apple, are you okay?" Mrs. Ruby grabbed my arm and looked into my eyes. "Did you hear what people are saying? Your work is spectacular. I'm just so glad that you finally agreed to show it."

"But I didn't." Tears filled my eyes as I overheard comments about my art. Yes, they were kind words, but they were words about a part of me that I hadn't planned to expose, that I hadn't prepared to have exposed. "I didn't agree to it."

"What do you mean?" Mrs. Ruby's eyes widened. "When Ty dropped it off, he said that you changed your mind. I thought

—" She took a sharp breath. "Oh no, Apple, I thought since the two of you had gotten so close that you'd asked him to bring it."

"Ty." A few tears slipped down my cheeks. Not only was I mortified that my art was on display, but now I had to deal with the fact that I'd begun to cry in front of a crowd of people.

"Apple!"

I heard his voice as I reached for my painting. A surge of fury mixed with adrenaline rushed through me.

"You!" I spun to face him with my painting in my arms. "How could you do this to me? How could you?"

"I thought it was so beautiful that it deserved to be shown. I just wanted you to have a chance to get a real opinion of your artwork—from people who know." He reached for my elbow.

I jerked it away and glared at him. "You had no right to do this!"

"I didn't know you would be this upset. I'm sorry." He reached up to swipe a tear away from my cheek with his thumb.

For a moment, I entertained the idea of smashing the painting over the top of his head. But instead, I turned and ran. I ran for the nearest door I could find, awkwardly attempting to keep the painting in my hands. As my chest burned with anger and hurt, I wished that I'd never met Ty, that I'd never looked into those light blue eyes and imagined that a good person was hidden behind his oversized hoodie and skateboard.

I pushed my way through one of the doors and out into the courtyard. As I sucked down deep breaths of air, my entire body trembled. I retreated to the very building I'd painted.

What if Maby saw it? What if the others did? They would be so upset that I'd exposed our secret. They would be so angry.

I burst through the door of the building to find it mercifully empty. I propped the painting up against a wall, then sank down into the cushions scattered across the floor. The tears that poured out of me were about more than just my painting hanging on the wall for everyone to see. They were for the praise I'd heard. They were for the artist inside of me that I'd felt pressured to hide and ignore.

Most of all, they were for the love I thought I shared with a boy I'd never expected to fall for.

TWENTY-NINE

Minutes slipped by, but the tears continued to flow. I wished I could just fade away, never to be seen again. Anything to escape the embarrassment I'd just experienced.

When I felt a hand on my shoulder, I jumped and gasped.

"Shh, it's just me." Ty sprawled out beside me, his hand still on my shoulder.

"You shouldn't be here." I glared at him and wiped at my eyes.

"I know. I know you probably hate me." He looked at me, his voice weighted with emotion as his fingertips coasted along the tears that streamed down my cheek. "I couldn't stand the thought of you being alone. You can hate me if you want to, Apple, but please, let me stay."

"Do I have a choice?" I took a breath and shivered as the warmth from his fingertips soaked into my skin. "You don't seem interested in letting me make my own decisions."

"I'm sorry." He squeezed his eyes shut, then frowned. "I messed up, Apple." He opened his eyes again and met mine. "I'm so sorry. I really wanted you to have a chance to see what people actually thought about your art. I didn't want you to hide anymore. I thought I was doing the right thing for once."

"So you stole my artwork and put it into a show without my permission and didn't even bother to tell me?" I pulled away from his touch as he attempted to stroke my cheek again. "Stop it!"

"I'll stop." He sat up and ran his hands back through his hair. "I tried to tell you. I called and I texted. Didn't you get them?"

"Of course I got them." I sat up as well, though I did my best to keep my distance from him. Just his presence was enough to confuse me. I wanted to hate him, but when he looked at me, I didn't feel hatred. Not even close. "I ignored them."

"I know you're upset with me." He shifted a little closer. "Maybe you can't have feelings for someone like me, someone who's so different from you."

"It's not about our differences." I locked my eyes to his. "It's about the lies you told. It's about hiding everything and then expecting me to just be okay with it."

"I'm not the only one that's been hiding things." He quirked his eyebrow as he stared back at me.

"That's just it, Ty. I can't trust you. Yes, maybe I didn't tell you who I was, but I had my reasons for that. You didn't tell me what you were doing because you knew it was wrong."

"No." He narrowed his eyes. "That's not true. I didn't tell you what I was doing, because I didn't think you would understand. Then, when I finally thought you might, when I did trust you, you just proved me right. You don't understand. Maybe you can't ever understand."

"Fine, I'm the problem." I stood up, then shook my head. "Don't worry about it. None of this matters. You can apologize all you want, but what you did today is unforgivable. I don't want to ever see you again. You don't belong here." I pointed to the door. "Get out."

"Now you wait just a second." His hand encircled my wrist, his touch gentle but his voice stern. "I'm sorry—so incredibly sorry if I upset you. I'm sorry if I hurt you." He took a slow breath. "I would never want to do anything to hurt you. But I'm not sorry that I made sure your art was out there for everyone to see. It shouldn't be hidden. You shouldn't be so scared of your own talent. So no, I don't regret doing what you should have been brave enough to do on your own. If you never want to see me again, that's your choice, but maybe I was around long enough to teach you how to be brave."

"Teach me how to be brave?" I yanked my hand out of his grasp and glared at him. "Is that what you call running from the cops? Is that what you call pretending to be a good guy around all the kids? Is that brave?"

"I would never do anything to hurt those kids!" He frowned.

"No? What if Patrick had seen you running from them? What do you think he would take from that? If he thinks that you think it's the right thing to do, then maybe he should do it too? Only Patrick isn't going to have anyone to bail him out of jail, is he, Ty?" I walked toward him as he glanced away. "That's right. He's not going to have some scared girl come to his rescue."

"I didn't ask you to." He whispered his words without looking up at me.

"No, you would never be brave enough to do that. You would never be brave enough to tell me the truth about what you were up to, because you'd be too scared that I would talk you out of it. So don't pretend that you're not just as scared, just as lost as I am." I bit into my bottom lip as he looked up at me. The fear I read in his eyes made my chest tighten with grief. Maybe I'd gone a little too far.

"Apple, please. Just give me a chance. You've never really given me a chance."

"Do you really think that?" I touched his cheek as I looked into his eyes.

"I do." He tilted his head toward mine.

I felt it too. I felt the urge, like a freight train running through me—the desire to forget all the pointless words we'd exchanged and lose ourselves in a kiss, a kiss I hoped would never come to an end.

I held my breath as his lips neared mine, then turned my head away at the last moment.

"No. Ty, you're the one that has never given yourself a chance." My hair fell forward to shelter my face from his probing eyes. "Please, I need to be alone."

"Apple, it doesn't have to be this hard." He took a step back. "We could just be together. We could just forget everything." He held his hand out to me. "Just ask me to stay and I'll show you. I'll show you that I can be the kind of person you want me to be."

"No." I brushed my hair back behind my ear and met his gaze with a stern glare. "You can't possibly be the kind of person I want you to be."

"Because I'm not rich?" He frowned. "Because my hair isn't cut right? Because my clothes aren't nice enough?" He crossed his arms. "I thought you were different than that."

"Because you aren't brave enough to really be you." I walked past him toward the door. "Stay if you want to. I don't care. But don't let Maby catch you here. You haven't been invited in."

"Apple, we're not done talking about this." He wrapped his arm around my waist just before I could reach the door. "I can try harder. Just give me a chance."

"I want to be with someone I can trust, Ty." I brushed his

hand off my waist and glanced over my shoulder at him. "I'm sorry. I don't want to hurt you either. But that seems to be all we do to one another. We should take that as a sign that this just isn't supposed to happen."

As I spoke each word, I wished I could take each one back.

I could see the pain in his eyes as he looked at me, then turned away.

I could feel that same pain ripple through me.

A single kiss could make it all go away. We could forget everything. We could ignore all the warning signs. But he'd already shown me the danger of being arrested, the danger of having myself exposed. He was a risk I just couldn't take. Maybe he wasn't grateful for the opportunity he had, but I was, and I had fought hard to try to keep it.

I stepped outside and fought the urge to turn back.

Of course I wasn't brave, I was terrified—terrified of never having the chance to be with him.

THIRTY

I slipped back into my dorm room and hoped that Candy wouldn't be there. Luckily, I found the living room empty and heard no music coming from my roommate's room. That was a good sign that she wasn't home. I didn't want to have to explain my swollen eyes or to face the knowledge that she'd heard about my artwork being in the show. I just needed a little time to think.

As I closed the door to my bedroom, I tried to force the memory of Ty's arm around my waist out of my mind. But as soon as I sat down on the edge of my bed, it returned.

My stomach flipped with the thought of his lips nearing mine.

Yes, I still wanted him. But I couldn't figure out why. He'd been cruel to me by putting my artwork in the show without my permission. He'd risked everything to paint a mural on a wall and then run from the police when he'd been caught.

I'd never had any interest in anyone who broke the rules, and yet, thoughts of him swirled through my mind.

Maybe this was my rebellious stage. My mother had been

promising me that I would go through it at some point in my life. Since I was a little girl, she'd warned me that one day I would want everything that wasn't good for me.

Was that why I wanted Ty?

I closed my eyes and tried to force him from my mind. It seemed like the harder I tried to forget him, the stronger the memories were. Memories of his words, his touch, even his scent.

I shuddered as the force of my desire for him coursed through me.

"Why?" I sprawled out across my bed and squeezed my eyes shut even tighter. As his words played through my mind, it felt like I was hearing them for the first time.

He wanted my work to be seen. He wanted me to be seen. Wasn't that what I really wanted? Somewhere deep inside me?

A knock on my bedroom door made my heart leap into my throat. For an instant I hoped that it was Ty. Maybe he would insist that I admit what I really wanted. Maybe he would pull me into his arms and kiss me.

As I walked over to the door, I realized that if he did kiss me, I would kiss him right back. I would kiss him, even if it made no sense, even if I regretted it, even if I hated myself for it.

My lips tingled as I pulled open the door.

Instead of Ty, Maby pushed her way inside.

"You can't hide out in here forever." She planted herself in the chair at my desk, then looked at me. "We need to talk."

"Is this about the painting?" I felt my cheeks grow even hotter. Even though she hadn't been aware of my thoughts right before I'd opened the door, they still swirled through my mind along with a hint of disappointment.

"I saw it at the hideout, after hearing about it from Candy and Alana. They were both at the show." She crossed one leg over the other and sat back in her chair.

"I'm so sorry, Maby. I never wanted anyone else to see that painting. I never thought that Ty would do something so crazy." I sat down on the edge of my bed as tears threatened again. "I know I messed up. I know I put everything at risk."

"I saw Ty at the hideout too. Did you invite him there?" She narrowed her eyes.

"No, I didn't." My heart dropped as I realized that she might think I wasn't being truthful. "He followed me one day. And he'd seen the painting." I held my breath for a moment, then exhaled. "Which I never should have painted in the first place. I'm so sorry. You trusted me and I've ruined everything."

"Apple." She leaned toward me and took one of my hands in hers. "The painting was amazing. I loved all the little details. I even spotted the couple on the roof. Maybe it is a risk, but it's one you felt you needed to take in order to express yourself." She shook her head. "I'm not angry. No one has mentioned anything about it. Mick has been stationed there all afternoon and no one out of the ordinary has shown up. I'm not here because of the painting—well, not exactly. I'm here because of you. When I found Ty, he was beside himself, certain that he'd destroyed everything between the two of you."

"He talked to you about it?" My eyes widened.

"Yes. A little. Then he took off on that skateboard of his." She rolled her eyes. "Look, love can be really complicated. But that doesn't mean that you should throw it away."

"How would you know?" The words popped out of my mouth and instantly I regretted them. The look on Maby's face told me that she'd taken them personally. "I'm sorry, Maby. I just meant—"

"No, you're right." She drew a deep breath. "I've made no secret of the fact that I'm not interested in dating while I'm in high school. Most of the couples I see lose themselves in puppy love, and when it all comes to an end—because it never should have started in the first place—it hurts. It leaves people devastated. It makes it impossible to concentrate on school, work, or friends. Lately, I've noticed everyone starting to pair up. It gets a little lonely to be me these days." She smiled, then shook her head. "But just because I don't know what it's like to be in love, that doesn't mean I don't know about love or know it when I see it. You and Ty may have some things to work out and it may be a little scary, but that doesn't mean that you should just run away. Or hide out in your room."

"Maby, I watched him get arrested. You don't know the whole story."

"I do." She smiled. "I know everything that happens around here, especially with my friends. I'm not going to lie to you about it. Ty takes risks that maybe he shouldn't. But he doesn't take those risks just for the thrill, does he? He takes them for a reason." She stood up from the chair and looked into my eyes. "It's easy to tell yourself all the reasons why he's wrong, why all this is his fault, but none of those reasons will mean anything a few weeks from now or a few months from now, when you realize that you let something truly special slip through your fingers."

"You really do know everything." I frowned as fear swept over me at the thought. Could I go a few months or even a few weeks with my lips still aching for Ty's kiss? What if I had to witness him with someone else? Could I handle that?

"Not as much as you may think." Maby frowned, then hugged me. "Think it through, Apple, that's all I'm saying. Think about what you really want, not just what you've been taught you should want or not want. Good luck." She paused at the door of my room and looked back at me. "I know it's not easy. But please know that I think your painting is beautiful, and for what it's worth, I think it deserves to be on display."

As she stepped out of my room, I felt a hint of pride swell up and grow stronger with each second it lingered.

Maby liked the painting? That meant more to me than she could ever know. Without Ty's deciding to submit my work to the show, I never would have experienced that proud moment.

THIRTY-ONE

I spent the rest of the weekend doing exactly what Maby told me not to do—hiding out in my room. Even when Candy knocked on the door and begged me to come out, I didn't.

I needed to protect myself from even the slimmest possibility of running into Ty or anyone who'd seen my artwork. Still, every time my phone buzzed, I checked to see if it was from him. When I saw that it wasn't, disappointment sent me right back to my bed. It made no sense to me that I didn't want to see him but still hoped he might text or call. The confusion was enough to exhaust me.

I spent time sketching in an attempt to calm my emotions. I sketched images of myself as a child with my favorite easel. I sketched images of my parents as they smiled for the press. I hadn't been given a choice when I was born to parents who were famous. No one asked me if I wanted to be part of such a lavish, but also limiting, lifestyle.

Of course if I ever opened my mouth to complain, I was told how grateful I should be. Not unlike the way I thought of Ty. He'd been given a luxury that most in his position would not receive and he should be grateful for it too.

"Grateful." I muttered as I sketched an image of myself hiding behind a curtain while my parents toasted to another great investment. They wanted me to be safe. That's why I had to hide, but no matter the reason, hiding had always been my way of life.

I shivered at the memory of seeing my painting on the wall and the way I'd reacted to it. I cringed and pulled the blanket up over my head. Yes, it seemed best never to leave my room again.

By the next morning, however, I had no choice. If I didn't go to class, I could end up on academic probation and that would do nothing to help my already tenuous academic situation.

I forced myself into a shower, pulled on my uniform, then trudged toward the art classroom. I didn't want to eat breakfast. I didn't want to see my friends. I just wanted to go through the motions and crawl back into bed when I was done.

When I opened the door to the classroom, I found Mrs. Ruby at my easel. Her eyes widened when she saw me.

"Oh, Apple, I'm so sorry again. I really had no idea, I really didn't."

"It's okay, Mrs. Ruby." I forced myself to smile. "I'm okay."

"I'm sure you're not." She hugged me. "I never would have done that to you, I hope you know that."

"I do. It was Ty who did it." I pulled away from her and cringed as I mentioned his name.

"I'm sure he was only trying to help." She met my eyes. "He wasn't wrong, you know."

"He wasn't?" I stared at her.

"What he did was wrong, yes, but he wasn't wrong about the idea of you sharing your work. I have so many people interested in your art." She held out a pile of business cards. "Each one of these people is interested in seeing more of your work. I do hope that you will contact them."

"Mrs. Ruby, I love art. I love creating it." My chest tightened as I continued. "But it's just a hobby. It's something I do just for myself. It's not for the world to see."

"I think the world feels differently." She winked at me then headed back to the front of the classroom. "Oh, and don't worry about running into Ty here, I had him switched out of this class. I thought after what he did it wouldn't be fair to you to have him here."

"Thank you." I walked over to the storage room to collect a few bottles of paint.

Although it was kind of Mrs. Ruby to make such an effort to protect my feelings, I couldn't deny the disappointment that I felt. I wanted to see Ty again, even though I had a million reasons not to.

As I selected my paint from the shelf, I remembered how close we'd come to a kiss when he'd joined me in the closet. I remembered how much I wished it would happen. Now it never would.

I turned and stepped out of the closet just in time to bump into Alana.

"Where have you been?" Alana raised an eyebrow. "I didn't see you in the cafeteria all weekend."

"I wasn't feeling so great." I shrugged and tried to step past her.

"Wait a minute." She stepped in front of me. "What's going on? I know that I'm not clued into everything that goes on in our little group of friends, but I can tell when something is wrong."

"I don't want to talk about it." Again I tried to step around her.

"Is it about Ty?" She stepped in front of me again. "I saw him outside in the courtyard when I came to class. I thought maybe he was waiting for you."

"Are you sure?" I was tempted to run right out to the courtyard to check.

"I didn't ask, but he didn't seem interested in moving, and it seemed to me that he was looking for someone." She met my eyes again. "Are you sure you're okay?"

"I will be." I sighed as I walked back to my easel.

Maybe Ty was waiting for me. Maybe he wanted another chance to explain himself, to apologize or not apologize. But why did he want that? Now that he knew who I was, who my parents were, how would I know if he was actually interested in me or interested in all that being with me entailed?

"It shouldn't even matter." I glared at the blank canvas in front of me. I'd slipped for a second. I'd imagined what it would be like to be with him again. But I couldn't let myself fall down that hole. I had to stay strong.

I repeated this mantra as I painted. It wasn't until the bell for the end of class rang that I realized what I'd painted. Ty, with his spray paint in one hand, his hoodie covering his face, and a blank wall in front of him.

"Great." I groaned and sat back on my stool.

He'd invaded more than just my life and my heart, he'd invaded my artwork.

I covered up the painting and hurried out of the classroom. For the rest of the day I remained determined to avoid any thoughts of him. This proved nearly impossible, however, as everyone wanted to bring him up.

At lunch, Maby asked me about him. In gym, Mick wanted to know why he hadn't met up with him for a run that morning. By the time I walked away from Oak Brook Academy, I was eager to stay away as long as possible.

As I headed for the bus stop, I felt a small pinprick of hope that he might be there. I doubted that after being picked up by the police, he'd be allowed to continue his community service hours at an elementary school. But maybe, just maybe, he would be there. Maybe he would have something to say to me.

Or maybe he would just kiss me.

I sighed as I reached an empty bus stop.

When I settled in a seat on the bus, I thought about what it had been like to have him sit beside me. I missed his presence—the faint scent of his shampoo and the way he would always glance at me when he thought I couldn't see him.

My heart ached when I stepped off the bus and walked into the school. I wanted him to be there beside me, joking and talking about the project for the day, bragging about Patrick's newest work.

How would I explain to Patrick that Ty wasn't coming back when I couldn't even understand it myself?

THIRTY-TWO

I did my best to smile through the class. But I felt a lot more like Patrick, who sat in the back of the classroom with a toy truck that he was bashing against the wall.

"Patrick, do you want to run the tires through some paint and see what you can create with it?" I crouched down beside him.

"No." He didn't look at me. He smashed the truck into the wall again.

"What about throwing some sponges? Want to do some of that? I can set up some paper for you..." I smiled.

"No!" He glared at me. "Just leave me alone."

"Patrick, why don't you tell me what's wrong, hon?" I tried to meet his eyes. "I know that Ty would want you to—"

"Ty isn't here!" He threw the car down. "He isn't ever going to be here again, is he?"

"I'm not sure." I frowned. I knew what the answer probably was, but I didn't have the heart to tell him that.

"I don't want to be here either." He picked up his truck and turned toward the door.

"Patrick, you can't just leave." I followed after him.

"Why not? Ty did." He shrugged and opened the door.

"If I have to get the principal to come, you could get into trouble." I frowned as I stepped in front of him.

"So?" He sighed as he looked down at the truck in his hand. "I'm always in trouble."

Something about the way he spoke reminded me of the way Ty spoke—guarded, already prepared for the worst.

"I'm sure that's not true. You're a great kid."

"No, I'm not. Everyone says I'm not. Everyone but Ty. Now he's gone." He shrugged. "He's a liar anyway, right?"

"Why would you say that?" I studied the anger in his expression.

"He said I was good at something. He must be a liar." He shoved his truck in his pocket. "I don't want to be part of this stupid club anymore."

"You are good at something." I looked straight into his eyes. "Patrick, you're good at a lot of things. You shouldn't listen to people that tell you different." My heart ached as I saw the pain in his eyes. He was so young to carry so much hurt. "I'll tell you what, if you stick around today you can mix paints—make any color you want, okay?"

"Really?" He perked up a little bit. "I don't have to do anything else?"

"Nothing else." I set some bowls of paint out for him on one of the tables.

As he began to mix the paints together, I watched him relax.

All at once I understood what Ty had said to me. Art was for everyone. It was easy for me to agree with that when I had been painting all my life. But until Patrick had become part of the art program, he might not have had much opportunity to paint. Now, just mixing the paints together gave him a sense of peace that he probably didn't have anywhere else in his life.

Maybe Ty's life had been that way too.

I closed my eyes as I remembered the sight of him running from the cops. He hadn't run because he'd wanted to get away, he'd run because he was scared. The same way that I'd run away from him. The same way I'd run from the art show. Maybe it wasn't wise for him to run, but maybe it wasn't a choice he'd made. Maybe he'd just been too scared not to.

With my heart in my throat, I left the school that evening.

I couldn't get the thought of Ty's being alone out of my mind. I remembered what he'd said to me when he found me in the hideout. He'd said that he didn't want me to be alone. Even though he knew I'd be angry at him, he still wanted to make sure that I wasn't alone.

All day people had asked me about him—wondering where he was, why he hadn't shown up for certain things—and it hadn't occurred to me what that meant.

It meant that he'd spent the day alone—with no one to make sure that he was okay.

Yes, my heart had been broken, but what if his was too? What if he really did care for me as much as he claimed? If he felt the same pain that I did and had no one to turn to, how could he handle it?

I didn't want him to be alone.

I spent the next hour looking for him. I checked the areas he liked to skateboard in. I checked the football field. I even hunted down Mick and his friends. But no one had seen him.

The more I searched, the more concerned I became that something serious might have happened. What if he'd decided to give up and walk away from everything? Maybe he would never come back to Oak Brook. The thought knocked the wind from my lungs.

With only one place left to look, I had to break a rule. Leaving school grounds after dark without a buddy was not allowed, but I needed to know that Ty was okay. If that meant getting into a little trouble, I would have to deal with it.

As I walked in the direction he'd taken me not long before, I wondered what I would do when I saw him. Would I speak to him? Would I be brave enough?

I heard the sound of the spray paint before I saw him. He wore a glow stick around his neck to give him just enough light to create. The faint light spilled over his face in a way that took my breath away. I watched as he moved swiftly and sharply, his arm thrashing through the air to create what he had in mind.

"Ty." I stepped up behind him. The draw of his presence made it impossible for me not to speak to him.

But the same did not seem to apply to him, as he continued to create, ignoring me.

I felt a pang of hurt as I realized that maybe he was right to ignore me. I'd been ignoring him after all. Even if he didn't speak to me, I was relieved to know that he was okay—more than okay. Apparently, it hadn't bothered him much at all, as he was right back to committing crimes.

My hands balled into fists at my sides. I had fallen for it again—the idea that he could actually care about me as much as I cared about him.

I turned to walk away and was almost at the end of the alley when I felt his hand on my shoulder.

"Apple!" He tugged the earbuds out of his ears as I turned to face him. "What are you doing out here alone?"

"I'd ask you the same, but I can see what you're doing." I glared at him. "You skipped school and now you're breaking the law? Are you just hoping the cops will come and arrest you again?"

"Apple, you don't understand." He frowned as he put his hands on my shoulders and looked into my eyes.

"I understand just fine. I understand because I was the one

who had to face Patrick today when you weren't there. I was the one that had to see him let down, because you can't just follow the rules or be grateful for what you've been given!" I grabbed his wrists, but I didn't pull his hands away from my shoulders.

The moment I touched his skin, all the anger that flooded through me was replaced with a surge of desire. I didn't want to yell at him. I wanted to pull him into my arms and hold him.

"Just look, alright?" He spun me around to face the wall and held up the glow stick. "Look what they did!"

My stomach churned as I saw the graffiti scrawled across his mural, splashed over the artwork of the children that he'd so carefully recreated. When he turned me back toward him, I could see the agony in his eyes.

"You don't understand, you can't."

THIRTY-THREE

"Then explain it to me." I crossed my arms as I stared at him. "Maybe instead of pushing me away, you could just tell me."

"What's the point?" He looked into my eyes. "You'll just run away."

"I'm not going anywhere."

"I'm supposed to believe that?" He tipped his head toward mine and lowered his voice to a whisper. "How can I? You've been running from me this whole time."

"Ty, I just want to know what's going on inside you. I want to understand why you would risk everything that you've been given here—your entire future—just to paint something on a wall!" I took his hand and gave it a gentle tug. "Show me, Ty. Show me why this is so important to you."

"Yes, I was given a great opportunity." He narrowed his eyes. "Not because I did something special, not because I was smarter than anyone else, but because I can run fast and throw a football. So I got plucked out of the struggle and dropped into this mansion of a school filled with people that know nothing about me and will never be able to understand where I've come from. And yes, people have been nice enough to me even though I'm different. The football team has taken me under their wing and Mick has been especially good to me. But that doesn't change the fact that none of these people have ever known what it's like to beg for food or to wonder if it would be the last night they'd sleep in a bed instead of in the street. So no, they can't understand."

"Ty, is that something you really experienced?" I stared into his eyes. "Did you really have to beg for food?"

"Yes, I did. I spent a lot of time wondering if we would have enough money for groceries, for the bills, how long the power would be cut off for." He frowned as he looked at me. "I know it's not your fault that I faced these problems and I know it's not your fault that you didn't, but you can't just expect me to forget and focus only on being grateful. Yes, I am grateful that I had this opportunity, but I also know that the rest of the kids living in those same circumstances—they aren't going to get a scholarship to Oak Brook Academy. They aren't going to get the opportunity that I did. I can't just pretend that I don't know that." He glanced back at the mural and sighed. "I just wanted them to have one thing they could look at, one thing they could see and know that they created something that they could be proud of—something that can't be taken from them. But look." He gestured to the graffiti that covered half of the mural. "It didn't work."

"Oh, Ty." I ran my hands along his shoulders as I stepped up behind him and looked past him at the mural. "I'm so sorry. I know you've been trying to explain this to me, but I didn't really understand it—not until today. You were able to reach Patrick because you understood him in a way that I didn't. I wish I'd been able to reach him in the same way."

"How is he?" He looked over at me.

"He misses you." I stared into his eyes. "We all do."

"You miss me?" He slid his arms around my waist and didn't hesitate to pull me close. "Is that true?"

"It's true." Breathless, my heart pounded as he studied me. "Ty, I'm still not happy about what you did. You shouldn't have put my art in the show without my permission."

"Art is for everyone. It's meant to be seen. It should be everywhere. I don't want you to keep it hidden away."

"And I don't want you to get arrested or kicked out of school." I searched his eyes. "Ty, I understand why you do it. I think. But this is too big a risk to take. With my parents being who they are, my landing behind bars would be a huge scandal that they might not be able to recover from. You're right that it's unfair that not every child gets the same opportunities, but that's just the world we live in. I live in a world that forces me to hide because my parents draw far too much attention. I have never—and most likely will never—have to worry about money. I've never gone hungry. I've never been without material things or a bed to sleep in. But I have been scared to be seen my entire life."

"Then change it." He touched my cheeks and looked deep into my eyes. "Stop it now. Be who you are, without fear, without hesitation—be brave."

"I will." My heart skipped a beat as I realized that I meant it. "But first you have to promise me that you won't put yourself at risk by breaking the law. You have to promise me that you will never run from the police again."

"Apple." He groaned and closed his eyes.

"Please, Ty." My chin trembled as the force of my emotions threatened to overwhelm me. "I can't see that again, I can't."

"I'm sorry." He slid his hands past my cheeks and through my hair to cup the back of my head. "I don't want to scare you."

As those words left his lips, the alley lit up in flashes of red and blue. A shrill siren chirped repeatedly as the police car made its way into the alley.

"Ty?" I gasped as the headlights of the police car shined into my eyes.

"I'm here." He grabbed my hand and squeezed it. "I'm right here, Apple, I'm not going to run."

My hand in his made me feel a little braver, but I still wanted to hide as the two officers stepped out of the car. Each one shined a flashlight—one at Ty and one at me. I shivered with fear as one of the officers paused in front of me.

"Doing a little artwork, are you?" He shined the flashlight on the graffiti that covered the mural.

"No, sir." Ty looked over at him. "No, she had nothing to do with this."

"And I'm supposed to believe that, Ty?" The other officer glared at him. "Didn't we just go through this? What did I say to you the last time I picked you up son?"

"You said it better be the last." Ty stared hard at the ground.

"Yes, that is what I said." He shined the light right into Ty's face. "So why are we back here again?"

"Why don't you go after the person that did that?" I pointed to the scrawled graffiti that covered Ty's beautiful art. "Why don't you hassle someone who is destroying something instead of spreading beauty?"

As the words left my lips, I felt shock set in. Had I really just spoken that way to a police officer?

"We enforce the law equally, young lady." The officer in front of me chuckled. "Unless you own this wall, it's illegal for anyone to be creating anything on it, beautiful or otherwise. The law doesn't care."

"Apple, it's fine." Ty shot me a sharp look and squeezed my hand. "Just take me in, officers." He released my hand and held his wrists out in front of him. "Like I said, she had nothing to do with it."

"She's here." The officer who stood in front of me grabbed me by the arm. "That's enough reason for me."

"Don't you touch her!" Ty started to lunge in the direction of the officer, but his hands were already trapped in the cuffs that the officer in front of him snapped on.

"Stop it, Ty, before you make things worse." The officer glared at him and tugged him toward the police car.

My heart flipped as I felt the cuffs tighten around my wrists.

Could this really be happening?

THIRTY-FOUR

As soon as the doors to the police car closed, Ty shifted toward me.

"I'm sorry, Apple. I'm so sorry. I'll do my best to get you out of this." His eyes widened as he stared at me. "I swear, I never thought that you could get caught up in all this. I never would have done it if I thought this might happen to you."

"Quiet back there!" One of the officers glared at us in the backseat.

I shrunk down in my seat and closed my eyes. It wasn't until Ty nudged me with his shoulder that I realized I'd been holding my breath for far too long.

"It's okay." He tried to meet my eyes. "Just breathe, it's going to be okay."

"It's not going to be okay." I glared at him. "You say I don't understand, but you don't understand either. This is not going to be okay." I sighed and closed my eyes again.

I wished I could just disappear. Hiding would not be enough when my parents found out about this. In fact, I was certain that they would never let me out of their sight again.

As tears built up in my eyes, I tried to imagine what I might be doing right at that moment if I'd never said two words to Ty. I'd probably be in my dorm room, watching a movie with Candy and pigging out on ice cream and popcorn. Instead, I found myself breathing in the scent of things that I couldn't even identify in the back of a police car.

I felt the tightness of the handcuffs as they dug into my skin.

Ty leaned his head against the window on his side of the car and stared out.

I saw his reflection in the glass of the window. I saw the hopelessness in his expression.

Maybe I was in a lot of trouble, but Ty was the one who would lose everything. He was the one that would likely be stuck in jail, lose his scholarship, and maybe even have no home to go back to. Sure, his behavior had led to it, but his behavior was motivated by something more pure and beautiful than I'd ever been able to paint. Maybe if I'd paid more attention to that in the first place, instead of judging him for his choices, I would have been able to prevent all this.

Ty took risks he didn't need to—there was no question there —but he took those risks because he believed they were the right things to do. When it came down to it, just like Patrick, Ty needed love. He needed to know that someone understood him and was in his corner.

I bit into my bottom lip as I realized how much time I'd spent thinking about myself and the angry parents I would have to face. It would be nothing compared to what Ty would find himself faced with.

"Ty." I shifted closer to him.

"You were right." He whispered his words, maybe because he didn't want to alert the officers in the front seat, but probably because the weight of his emotions didn't allow him to speak any louder. "I did put you at risk. I never should have gotten involved with you. I promise, Apple, when this is all over, I'll stay out of your life."

"Ty, that's—" My words were cut short by the sharp bark of the officer driving.

"If I hear one more word out of either of you, I am going to make sure that you both end up in solitary."

I shivered at the thought. I didn't think the officer could actually follow through with that threat but knowing that didn't stop me from thinking about what it would be like. I glanced over at Ty, but he kept his eyes fixed on the window.

When we were led into the police station, I noticed that the officer who escorted me held my arm gingerly. The officer who escorted Ty had a strong grip and jerked him in the direction that he wanted Ty to go. As we were fingerprinted, everyone involved spoke to me respectfully. Ty's hand was twisted and shoved until they had every fingerprint they wanted.

"Don't give us any trouble tonight, my patience is already thin." The officer beside Ty glared at him.

"Yes, sir." Ty frowned. "But I'm the one that did the painting. Can't you see my hands are stained? Hers aren't."

"No?" The officer beside me grabbed my hand and held it up. There were speckles of paint all over it.

"It's from earlier today." Ty shook his head. "She didn't do anything to the wall."

"Nice try, kid, but it won't do you any good to try to protect your girlfriend." The officer shoved him toward the holding cell. Ty stumbled a few steps forward.

"She's not my girlfriend." He briefly met my eyes before he stepped inside the cell.

His words lashed against my heart. He was right. I wasn't. But I didn't like hearing him say it. I jumped as the holding cell door slammed shut.

"What about me?" I stared at the officer.

"You can take a seat over there." He pointed to a bench not far from the holding cell. "We've already got a call in to your parents."

Stunned, I sat down on the bench. It wasn't lost on me that Ty and I had been arrested for the same crime, and yet he was behind bars and I was on a bench with an officer removing my handcuffs.

"Can I call them?" I looked up at the officer.

"I think you'd better." He handed me a phone.

I stared at the phone for a moment. I knew once I made the phone call, I would have to admit the truth. I would have to tell my parents where I was and why. My heart pounded as I punched in the number. I had to do something to help Ty, even if it meant facing the wrath of my parents.

"Why are you at the police station?"

"Mom?" I gulped. "How did you know where I was?"

"The officer called me when he picked you up, Apple. All of the police know that you attend Oak Brook and they keep an extra eye on you."

"Seriously?" I frowned.

"Of course. Did you think your father and I would just let you wander around on your own without protection? Honestly, I can't believe I'm dealing with this. Do you have any idea how much pressure your father and I are under right now? If news of this gets out, it could ruin everything!"

"I'm so sorry, Mom." I sighed. "I didn't mean for any of this to happen."

"I'm sure you didn't." Her voice softened some. "You just got involved with the wrong boy. I've warned you about that. But I guess we all have to go through it. I certainly hope that you've learned your lesson."

"Ty isn't a bad guy. He was really doing something great."

"None of that." Her voice sharpened. "I don't want to hear

another word about him, do you understand me? Now, your father and I are going to figure out a way to get you out of this. Just do your best not to talk to anyone."

"Mom, Ty is the one who really needs some help." I frowned.

"What did I say about mentioning his name? I know what he did. He's some kind of graffiti artist. Don't think I didn't hear about your artwork being in an art show at your school. We have a lot to talk about. Honestly, I thought you'd grown out of that art phase."

"It's not a phase!" I groaned.

"Stop, Apple. Don't be childish. We have to get this figured out."

I took a deep breath and closed my eyes. "I think I can help you with that."

THIRTY-FIVE

Within an hour my father arrived at the police station. I didn't have to be notified to know it. Many officers rushed to the front of the station and whispers rippled through the rest. I braced myself as I heard his heavy steps in the hallway.

"Apple." He stared at me as he neared me. "What happened here?"

"Dad, I just—"

He held up a hand before I could finish.

"Save it. It's already over." He pointed to the bench. "You stay right here. Don't move a muscle, understand?"

"Yes." I clenched my hands together and tried to hold back everything I wanted to say. I knew my family's policy about keeping personal discussions private. As I attempted to find words to explain what happened, I realized that he wasn't going to believe a word I had to say. I watched as he walked straight over to the holding cell.

Ty walked toward the bars as my father paused in front of them.

"So you're the reason my little girl ended up in the back of a police car?"

"Dad!" I stood up from the bench.

"Not a word!" He pointed his finger straight at me without looking away from Ty.

"Yes, sir. I'm sorry about all this."

"You should be." He glared at Ty. "I don't know what your story is and I'm not interested in it either. I'll tell you this once and you'd better listen. You are not to go anywhere near my daughter. Do you understand me?"

"Yes." Ty narrowed his eyes and took a step back from the bars. "Whatever you say."

"Exactly." My father smacked his hand against the bars, then turned to face me. "I told you not to move off that bench."

"But Dad, it's not Ty's fault."

"No, it's not. Because I've raised you to be smart enough not to get involved with a punk like that! I have more important things to be doing right now!" He brushed past me and stormed back through the police station.

I sank back down onto the bench and rested my head in my hands. Not long after my father left, an officer walked me to the door of the police station.

"I'm going to give you a ride back to Oak Brook." He pulled the door open.

"What about Ty?" I looked over my shoulder.

"He's being released as well, but your mother made it clear you were not to see him." He met my eyes. "Count yourself lucky, young lady. If it weren't for your parents, you'd be spending the night here and possibly longer." He led me outside into the parking lot. "If I were you, I'd listen to your mother. She's trying to protect you."

"Yes, sir." I nodded as I slid into the back seat of the police car.

I wanted to be grateful, but I just felt sick to my stomach. My mother had insisted that if she did what I asked, I would have nothing to do with Ty. I had to promise that I would stay away from him. But it was the last thing I wanted to do.

I wanted to find Ty, wrap him in my arms, and kiss away every bit of pain that he'd ever experienced. Instead, I walked through an empty courtyard toward the dormitory and tried not to think about where he might be.

When I stepped through the door of my dorm room, Candy stood up from the sofa to greet me with open arms.

"Oh, I was so scared!" She hugged me tight. "I heard about you being arrested. I'm so sorry, Apple, I can't believe that Ty pulled you into that. I'm sorry that I ever let you get involved with him."

"It wasn't his fault." I pulled away from her and flopped down on the sofa. "None of this was his fault. I was just too blind to see what was really going on with him."

"But he got you in trouble with the police!" She shook her head. "There's nothing forgivable about that."

"He didn't get me into trouble. I just happened to be there at the right time." I shivered at the memory of the handcuffs. "Candy, I had to call my parents to get us out."

"Ugh! Well, at least they got you out. I think my grand-mother would probably leave me to rot just to teach me a lesson." She rolled her eyes.

"I'm glad they got us out, but they wanted me to promise not to see him again. But all I can think about is seeing him." I picked up my phone and checked it. "I've sent him tons of texts and he's not answering me."

"Maybe that's for the best, Apple. You two—you don't have enough in common to make things work."

"I don't care about any of that. I only care about him. But now he probably thinks I hate him. My dad made him promise he wouldn't have anything to do with me. He's probably too scared to talk to me now." I tightened my grasp on my phone. "I don't know if he's coming back to Oak Brook. I don't have any idea where he is! It's driving me crazy."

"Girl, you just need to sleep it off." Candy crossed her arms. "I'm sorry, but I think your parents are right. Nothing good has happened since you've gotten involved with Ty."

"Nothing good?" I stared at her, my eyes wide. "Are you kidding me? The best part of my life has been the time I've spent with Ty. Something good has happened. He happened." I stood up and walked into my room.

As I closed my door, I felt frustration and panic flood through me. Candy couldn't even understand what I was feeling?

I understood in that moment how Ty must have felt at Oak Brook Academy. How alone and uncertain. I couldn't even imagine closing my eyes to sleep. Instead, I waited until I heard Candy's soft snores. If Ty wouldn't answer my calls, I would have to get my message across another way.

As I left the dormitory behind, I felt a faint rush of fear.

Yes, something in me had changed. I'd become brave.

THIRTY-SIX

It didn't take me long to find the same alley.

When I arrived, I felt a spark of hope that Ty might be there. But the alley was empty. More graffiti had been scrawled across Ty's mural.

Armed with cans of spray paint he'd left behind the night before, I began to restore the mural. It took some trial and error as I wasn't used to using spray paint, but after some time, I began to get the hang of it.

By the time I switched to my own supply of paints, the sky had begun to lighten with the promise of dawn. The smell of spray paint surrounded me and I could feel sticky spots in my hair and on my skin where the paint had landed. I painted my own final touch onto the mural, then took a step back to look at it.

"Apple!" Ty rushed toward me from the end of the alley. "What are you doing?" He grabbed the paintbrush out of my hand, and in the process, sent globs of gold paint flying. It splatted against my face and neck as he tried to wrench the paintbrush from my hand.

"Ty, it's okay, stop!" I let him take the paintbrush and took a step back. "Just calm down!"

"Calm down?" He glared at me. "How can I possibly do that? Are you trying to get yourself locked up again? How could you even try something like this after your parents got us out?"

"Ty, you don't understand." I glanced over at the mural. "Don't you like what I've done?"

He turned to face it, his eyes still narrowed. Then they widened.

"You did this?"

"I did. I know it's not as good as it was, but I'm not used to using spray paint and I did the best I could."

"It's different." He stared at the center of the mural. "You added something."

"It's you." I smiled as I pointed to the golden hair that peeked out of the edge of the hoodie that I'd painted on the wall. "The mural was missing you. Ty, I think your artwork is amazing and I think it deserves to be seen."

"Apple, it's beautiful." He stared into my eyes, then sighed. "But you still shouldn't have done it. It's too much of a risk."

"That's the thing. It's not." I smiled as I swept my hand along his cheek. "It's only illegal to paint on walls you don't own."

"What do you mean?" He frowned.

"I mean that's how my parents got us out. They bought the building. So now no one can arrest you for painting on it." I tipped my head toward the paintbrush in his hand. "You can paint anything you want, Ty, anything at all."

"You blow me away Apple, do you know that?" He dropped the paintbrush on the ground and cupped my cheeks with his hands.

"Ty." I sighed as I smiled. "I said that you could paint anything you wanted."

"I am. I'm painting the most spectacular masterpiece I've ever seen." He ran his palms through the paint that had landed on my cheeks and swept it over my skin until he reached the back of my neck.

Dizzy from the warmth of his touch, I almost didn't notice when his head tipped toward mine. I felt his fingertips press gently against the back of my head as his lips grew closer.

As my heart skipped a beat, I held my breath. Could this really be happening?

Just before his lips would meet mine, he paused. He hovered so close that I could feel his breath tickling against my skin.

"Apple." He whispered, his eyes locked to mine. "Breathe, you have to breathe."

Only then did I realize that I hadn't exhaled. As my breath drifted from between my lips, his closed the distance between us. The glide of his lips against mine inspired a rush in me that I'd never even known was possible. My heart raced faster than I could stand. My mind spun with a swift dizziness that threatened to knock me off my feet. Luckily, he held on tight. I understood then how a kiss could last forever.

Even as he broke away, breathless, his cheeks red and his eyes wide, the kiss remained. Time had stopped the moment that his lips touched mine and I was sure it would never start again, at least not in exactly the same way.

"Ty." I wrapped my arms around him and in the process paint was smeared from my cheek across his along with a few strands of his hair. "I promise, I won't hide from you anymore."

"I promise I won't run." He held me close as he whispered in my ear. "I promise I'll find a way to be with you, no matter what it takes."

"We can both be brave." I smiled as I pulled away enough to look into his eyes. "Can't we?"

"Absolutely." He pulled me close again. "Apple, I don't know what the future is going to bring, but I do know that you're going to be part of it. I don't know where I'm going once I leave Oak Brook Academy, but I'll find a way to stay close to you."

"Oh, you're not leaving." I grinned as I ran my hands through his hair. "I couldn't possibly let you go."

"What do you mean?" He laughed and squeezed his arms around my waist. "Are you going to hide me under your bed?"

"That's a good thought." I raised an eyebrow. "But no, that's not what I mean. My parents have their ways of getting me to do what they want, but I have my ways of getting them to do what I want too. I just told them that if you lost your scholarship to Oak Brook Academy, I would refuse to continue to attend."

"Apple!" He frowned. "Your father is going to hate me even more." He groaned.

"I don't care. He'll forget all about it once he has the chance to get to know you." I rested my cheek against his chest. "Ty, I'll do whatever it takes to make sure that your life is better from now on."

"It already is." He brushed the sleeve of his hoodie across my cheek and wiped away some paint. Then he tipped my head up toward his and looked into my eyes. "You brought beauty back into my world, Apple—real beauty, the kind that I almost stopped believing in. That's something I'll always be grateful for." He pressed his lips against mine and drew me into a passionate kiss.

As my knees weakened and the first bit of sunlight broke through the last of the night's darkness, I realized that I'd learned from Ty exactly what I'd longed to know all of my life—that no matter how scary the world was and how much I wanted to hide, sometimes taking a risk was worth everything and the only way to truly be happy.

EPILOGUE

"Apple?" Ty's voice echoed through the large empty building.

"Over here!" I called out to him as I struggled to get a board into place.

"Let me help you!" He rushed over and pushed the board into place for me. As he shook his head he grinned. "You never stop, do you? Don't you have an art class to get to?"

"Mr. Fein can wait." I winked at him as I wrapped my arms around him. "I just can't believe this is really happening. Can you?" I looked into his eyes.

"Of course I can." He stared back at me. "You dreamed it and then you created it. I knew you would have it the moment that you mentioned it."

"I just hope the opening goes smoothly." I glanced around at the large space. "Things are nowhere near ready."

"We have time." He placed his forehead against mine. "Have I told you how beautiful you are today?"

"Stop." I rolled my eyes. "I have paint and dust all over me."

"Not all over you." He dipped his fingertip into an open paint can near us. "But I can fix that!"

"Don't you dare!" I gasped and laughed as he chased me

through the building. As I neared the door, I collided with Maby, who had just stepped inside.

"Oof! Watch it!" She rolled her eyes. "What are you two doing? You know this isn't a place to play, right?"

"Isn't it?" Ty quirked an eyebrow as he tapped his paint-covered fingertip against Maby's nose.

"Stop!" She swatted his hand away. "Oliver, can you believe these two?" She glanced over her shoulder. "Oh, I guess you might need some help with those boxes, huh?"

"I'll help." Ty stole a quick kiss from me, then stepped out through the door.

My heart swelled with joy. Not only had Ty and I grown closer over time, we'd created a space that would soon be open to all the kids in the neighborhood. A place where they could paint on the walls, or throw balloons filled with paint at the ceiling. It was the same building my parents had purchased, but it was no longer empty. Now it would be filled with the laughter and creativity of hundreds of children, not to mention the student volunteers that would be taking turns supervising.

"You did it, Apple." Maby turned to look at me. "I'm not sure how, but you really did it. You can create miracles."

"It's a group effort." I smiled. "But it does feel good to know that soon it will be open. I can't wait to see what the kids come up with to create." I heard a crash, followed by a string of posh-sounding curse words. "Speaking of miracles." I locked my eyes to hers and took a step closer to her. "You seem to be spending an awful lot of time with Oliver."

"Don't!" She pointed her finger at me. "Don't you even go there!"

"I'm not!" I held up my hands innocently. "I'm not saying a word."

Ty stepped back inside and set a pile of boxes down on the floor. Then he grabbed me around the waist.

"I missed you."

"You were gone thirty seconds." Maby rolled her eyes.

"I missed you too." I smiled as I kissed him.

"Okay, I'll get the rest of the boxes." Maby threw her hands up into the air. "Anything to get away from this nonsense."

"Or maybe just to be alone with Oliver." I grinned as I whispered the words to Ty. "What do you think?"

"I think miracles really do happen. I also think that as long as they're out there, we're alone in here." He grinned as he pushed me up against the wall.

I wrapped my arms around his neck and pulled him in for a kiss. Things couldn't be better. I could hardly believe how much my life had changed since Ty had become a part of it.

ALSO BY JILLIAN ADAMS

Amazon.com/author/jillianadams

OAK BROOK ACADEMY SERIES

The New Girl (Sophie and Wes)

Falling for Him (Alana and Mick)

No More Hiding (Apple and Ty)

Worth the Wait (Maby and Oliver)

A Fresh Start (Jennifer and Gabriel)

Made in the USA
Coppell, TX
04 December 2021

67060864R00132